Seer

By
RICK MURCER

PUBLISHED BY:
Murcer Press, LLC

Edited by
Janet Fix, www.thewordverve.com

Interior book design by
Bob Houston eBook Formatting

www.rickmurcer.com

Seer © 2015 Rick Murcer
All rights reserved

This book is a work of fiction. The names, characters, places, and incidents are products of the writer's imagination or have been used fictitiously and are not to be construed as real. Any resemblance to persons, living or dead, actual events, locales or organizations is entirely coincidental.

ISBN: 0692432388

Seer

A Novel

By
RICK MURCER

To my wife Carrie. I love you as much today as ever.

Thank you for not giving up on me.

1-CHAPTER

I never saw it coming.

Not the roaring, out-of-control tractor trailer, the indescribable fear and pain, and most assuredly, not the inexplicable "gift" the accident would lavish upon my previously benign senses.

Perhaps "lavish" is somewhat paradoxical because it means to expend without limit, and my senses certainly have limits, or at least the "gift" seems to. Those limitations unquestionably could be my lack of understanding and leery unwillingness, and not the function of the bestowed gift. I'm pretty new at this "seeing" thing and what it brings to the proverbial table.

And I'm scared of it.

No, that's not quite right. Petrified works. As in pee-my-pants, get-the-spider-off- my-face, there's-a-freaking-snake-the-length-of-an-interstate-in-my-commode type of terror. Yeah, that fits.

I'd never thought of myself as someone afraid of much of anything. Seeing what I've seen over the last few hours has changed that, though. It would change you too.

But I'm getting ahead of myself. Let me bring you up to the moment in the best way a man with my unlikely background is able. I'll hurry, but I don't have much time.

None of us do.

My name is Gabe Stark. Actually, my parents named me Gabriel Andrew Stark—nice initials, eh? There isn't anything particularly special about me, at least in laymen's terms, until the accident changed my perception of what that idiom might potentially entail.

I can sing a little, played some sports, and I have a knack for keeping most folks relatively calm. The latter comes in handy in my line of work.

People who possess unusual athletic talent, incredible musical ability, or grand wealth seem to fulfill the criteria that "special" implies these days, and for that, I am grateful.

We—our society that is—needs all of them. Well, almost all of them. I don't watch Miley Cyrus or Tiny Tim videos any longer.

I suppose you could argue the merits of "special," yet I perceive the term as subjective and elusive to quantify as "chocolate ice cream tastes better than vanilla" or "my dad is tougher than your dad." It's difficult to beat chocolate anything, however.

Anyway, one week after my thirty-sixth birthday, I began my jaunt of six miles to our country home. I left around six thirty from my job as a bill collector at the Caring Collection Agency, geared up to engage one of the sudden, blinding December snowstorms that so often attack our quaint little town of North Haven along Northern Michigan's west coast.

Sometimes these storms bring a sense of excitement to the community, suffusing the good cheer of the season into a more memorable Christmas experience. I suppose, for some, it did exactly that. In retrospect, I wish it had been eighty degrees that evening.

As for my place of employment, I know what you're thinking. Caring Collection Agency? What hogwash! The name of our company may very well contain as diametrically opposed ideas as any in the English language. Kind of like signing up for one of those "all you can eat" pasta and candy diets that guarantee you'll lose five pounds a week. Or the idea that you can watch too much baseball. Or read too many books. None of those ideas compute. However, we are as real as our company name implies. We *do* care, but more about that later.

There were two weeks remaining until glorious Christmas morning, and I was contemplating what final gifts would be appropriate for my wife of ten years, Kara, and our chocolate Lab, Apollo.

We hadn't been able to conceive children over the years—not enough fish swimming upstream—so the dog and a boatload of orphans in the local orphanage were the fortunate recipients of our generous affections. The spoiled, oversized canine seemed to realize that fact better than the children in the home and played it to the hilt.

While we both love kids, we never really considered adoption because we always believed God would provide us a child when the time was right. We were wrong, and now, in our middle-aged minds and in our mid-thirties, we considered ourselves well past prime child-rearing energy. And kids take energy, right?

As the dancing, wind-driven snowflakes bounced from my windshield like an endless swarm of pallid insects, I cranked up the stereo and began to bellow out *The Christmas Song,* accompanying the incomparable Nat King Cole (who really didn't need my assistance, but hey, it was Christmas and I was in a charitable mood).

After a few bars, I looked into the rearview mirror and noticed the halogen lights of the vehicle behind me vacillating in a manner suggesting lack of control. Not a terribly encouraging sign on these icy, snow-swept roads at fifty miles per hour.

I kept my intense vigil as the vehicle grew closer and consequently larger, much larger, moving precariously closer to my red 2000 Ford Taurus, almost blinding me in the process.

The approaching vehicle was obviously a much bigger means of transportation than mine, and the fearful little feeling one acquires when panic replaces tension began rising up from somewhere south of my throat. I would later find out that it was a Chevy Tahoe being guided, or not guided, as it turned out, by a teenage driver who was trying to impress his companions with his newly-discovered ability to drive in winter weather. Did I say I love kids?

Backing off the accelerator in hopes that the driver of the vehicle behind me would realize the error of his way and slow down accordingly was my first mistake.

The unit picked up speed and now was literally inches from my bumper, eminent disaster for one or both of us just moments away. I considered tapping the brakes, but it could have done more harm than good. Moreover, what was wrong with the driver? Was he blind?

Nat was still crooning while I queried my options traveling an icy two-lane with a moronic driver behind the wheel of a large SUV fixing to become my car's proctologist . . . and maybe mine in the process.

Those options were few.

My perspiration was now beginning to outperform the holiday air freshener hanging from the mirror that had been odorizing the interior of my car with refreshing evergreen and tantalizing candy cane, and with good reason. There was only about a mile to go before we'd reach the busy, major intersection of Highway 62 and Highway 85.

The traffic light at this particular junction was notoriously slow to turn, and in this weather, the hue of the light meant much less than the velocity of oncoming traffic. San Francisco driving had nothing on the likes of rural Michigan traffic or its drivers. Right of way was more like a suggestion.

My eyes wider than a cartoon character's, I glanced to my left and could see a stream of headlights in the northbound lane, and to my right ranged a twelve-foot drainage ditch with steep banks and tall snow banks cascading into an intimidating "V." That's when the first recoil between bumper and trunk jolted me to the next level of terror. I guess that would be Terror Level Two.

"Oh God," I croaked.

I guess I was hoping my pathetic plea, reeking of unbeliever desperation, would send an instant army of God's angels to rescue me from whatever unpleasantries destiny seemed to have ordained for me.

One can hope. And I was hoping my derriere off.

The next glimpse was of my wavy red hair in the rearview mirror, and I wondered if it would still be attached to my scalp when this was over. Or even if my head would be, you know, still connected.

I wasn't overly optimistic.

The Taurus progressed into its horrifying, uncontrolled spin with my hands virtually squeezing the steering wheel into gray synthetic pulp. In the vernacular of my coworker, Abbey Manis, I was pretty much bent over two ways from Sunday.

According to some—experts, I suppose—time slows to an inexplicable creep in situations like this. I've read that it's the brain's way of helping the body to survive. Apparently my brain was tired of the rest of me because a slowing of my environment was the last thing I experienced. In fact, if things had moved any faster, I would have passed out.

I've always been pretty good at keeping my limited wits in tight situations, so my brain reminded me to do all of the things we were taught in the infamous drivers training course required of every high school student. I tapped the brakes, turned into the spin, swore like a sailor, and begged for the car to listen to my voice, blah, blah, blah. Nothing worked.

It became increasingly apparent that I needed an unanticipated miracle to avoid boatloads of pain . . . or worse. I then rushed to the most universal of defaults in times like these; I prayed like a man being ominously strapped into a Texas electric chair.

As if by some divine cue, or just sheer crappy driving by one or both of us, I received my answer almost immediately, in the form of another bone jarring thump to the Taurus's rear, compliments, of course, of the large vehicle traversing startlingly close to my slow-spinning Old Red.

Immediately after the spontaneous slam to the right quarter panel, Old Red straightened out and the spinning segment of my road adventure was complete. I was entirely grateful. Spinning and I don't get along.

I am one of those folks that can spontaneously puke by just helping some little tike stay steady for a couple revolutions on the playground's merry-go-round. Motion sickness and I have a deep-rooted love/hate relationship. I hate to puke, and it loves to make me.

In any event, I barely had time to blurt out the breath I had been jealously hoarding (one never knows when the opportunity to take another may present itself, and I was taking no chances) and to focus wide eyes through the snowy windshield.

I didn't care for what was next on my dance card.

This nightmare was spiraling into just that, a nightmare. I was no longer traveling along the intended route the engineer had designed for this shimmering, ice-covered asphalt ribbon. I was, instead, streaking out of control toward the twelve-foot trench that doubled as a drainage ditch, and perhaps, in this fastidious instance, a frigid underwater deathtrap.

I find it amazing how one's sense of positive thinking dissolves into a disciple of Murphy's Law under circumstances such as these. I, wanting not to offend the masses concerning that paradigm, knew without a fraction of misplaced doubt, death was waiting with open arms for me. Of course, I would first have to go through the ghastly act of striking the embankment and watching, in pointed, horrific, slow motion, as I sank slowly to the bottom of the frigid, watery trench.

Old Gabe could already feel his body temperature dropping twenty degrees. I suddenly wondered what my underwear would feel like in that environment.

Hey, think about it.

I then did what every able-bodied, macho man on the planet would resort to and covered my face, screamed like a terrified school girl, and waited for death's scythe to harvest yet another soul.

2-CHAPTER

In the past, when I heard of people talking about their lives passing in front of their eyes in perilous situations similar to my current predicament, I paid it little credence and passed it off as an urban legend or some old, less quantitative, wives' tale.

I hate being on a roll . . . because I was wrong again, dead wrong.

In the instant before impact, I saw much.

Hurts I had administered, wrongs I had delivered against people, some of whom I'd never really known, or at the very least, had forgotten. Intentional or not, I felt what those poor souls had felt.

My humiliation and shame were driven even deeper with the knowledge of selfish desires and ambitions that really had no defined purpose, other than to fulfill some self-centered impulse. Like, for instance, the incident with the peacock feathers and my grandfather's tractor. (There will *not* be more information forthcoming on that little episode.)

There were good things too. Wonderful apparitions. For one, meeting Kara, the very best thing to happen to me. Her undaunted support and influence coursed through my adult life with remarkable consistency.

I saw her enchanting, beryl-green eyes regarding me with such love that it startled me, as it often did.

That expression, that unexplainable gaze, impressed even more intently my nearly complete lack of understanding of why a woman with her undeniable physical beauty (she is hot) and unmatched gentleness could be drawn to someone as ordinary as I.

I heard once that we should never question the destinies that lure loving soulmates to one another, no matter what the relationship looks like to the rest of the world. I don't. Okay, maybe once, or three thousand times, but it doesn't make me any less grateful for her.

In other words, don't knock it.

Strangely, there also appeared, in this instantaneous reflection of my rather unremarkable existence, a very young, wonderful face accompanied by one much older, almost ancient.

They were both people I knew I'd never met, but each radiated such eccentric familiarity that both images caused my heart to jump. Not the heart that pumps blood—that one was surely jumping enough already—but the one that is purely undefinable emotion. We all have it. We all covet more of it, and paradoxically, we all seem to spend a lot of time denying it, at least to ourselves.

Yet, as my immediate circumstances would dictate, I really had no time to dwell on these unusual visualizations. My stream of life experiences and back-visions were abruptly interrupted by the loathsome collision I'd been anticipating.

The impact was . . . brilliant.

My head slammed forward at the same time my airbag deployed, countering the forward momentum of my somewhat prodigious noggin. I'm not great at physics, but even I knew this was going to hurt. Yep, it did.

I'm no boxer, but I felt like Mike Tyson had decided I was an IRS agent and began to rearrange my face. It wasn't just my pretty cheekbones either.

I heard popping and cracking as my vertebrae spoke, debating whether to put me in a wheelchair, end my life, or just make some spine-wrenching chiropractor the happiest person in the fine village of North Haven. I vaguely wondered if my insurance policy included clauses that cover prolonged ventures into the realm of natural healing, or would I be calling myself from the collection agency, demanding payment for unpaid treatments? Bizarre deliberations, I admit, but, as they say . . . well, who really cares what the hell they say?

That's what was going on in the old thought processes, for whatever reason.

With my head firmly encased within a nitrogen-filled nylon bag pressing entirely too fiercely, intimately sharing its somewhat putrid chemical odor with my face, I felt the car side-wind after the head-on kiss, strike the bank, and rise up on the two passenger-side tires like a cartoon scene from *Speed Racer*. (Isn't it curious how much he and Jeff Gordon look alike? They could be twins!)

There Old Red remained, balanced for what seemed like an eternity. I wondered what was taking so long and why fate was teasing me this way.

By then, there was almost no question that I'd be paralyzed from the neck down, so let's just get this debacle over with, right? But fate, as it turned out, had other plans. The car dropped, as gently and ceremoniously as possible, back down to four on the floor, crunching snow and ice while completing its unlikely journey to stability.

I took a few seconds to evaluate what just happened. Good God, I was alive. I hadn't rolled down the Valley of Ice. In fact, I didn't even hang on the precipice of the sinister "V" just feet away.

Maybe my desperate pleading to a God I didn't know had worked. Or maybe my Irish luck had finally worked for once. Either way, airbag and all, I knew I was alive.

A moment later, after one more trip down the road of thanksgiving, I made the hardest decision I'd made to date . . . well, other than evoking all my will not to wet myself. I decided to get out of Old Red, which meant I had to move my left leg— something a quadriplegic couldn't accomplish.

I gathered every ounce of intestinal fortitude and gave it my best shot. Nothing happened.

My mind ran berserk with thoughts regarding the difficulty, or lack thereof, in moving one's leg. After all, I had been doing it a hell of a long time, right? Unless, of course, one has lost all motor control and is destined to become dependent on wheelchairs, church ladies, and Meals on Wheels.

Not relishing the thought of Kara leaving me and being forced to beg for food, I gathered my remaining courage and attempted to wiggle my right toes. Yes! They frittered around my size-ten wingtip. My brain exploded with ecstasy, well sort of. At any rate, I had hope.

Bravery coursed through my veins like an illegal drug and I attempted, successfully, to move my arms and hands. Everything was working except for my left leg. Three out of four ain't bad.

I simply cannot describe the feeling of pure relief that moment rendered. Warm tears threatened. I manned-up and sent them packing, nearly.

By now the pallid airbag had deflated at a rapid pace, allowing my eyes access to the real world, and more importantly, more sweet air rushed to my lungs.

Reaching out my left hand with newfound confidence, I flicked on the dome light and could immediately see the reason my left leg hadn't responded to my effort. The emergency brake foot pedal had dropped down against my leg, pinning it fast against the inside firewall. Gingerly, and with less pain than I had anticipated, I reached the foot pedal's steel linkage and pulled. As I exerted increased effort, it gradually moved to the right, just enough, to allow my calf some well-earned freedom. I rubbed the pinched area and immediately thought that Thor would have been proud of my exhibition of super-human strength. On the other hand, he probably wouldn't have rubbed his calf with half the enthusiasm I had.

I took another moment to be thankful to God, or whomever may or may not be out there, for keeping me safe. I learned a long time ago to cover as many bases as possible, and I was now covering that one. One never knows, right?

There was no mistaken that I was here, and lucky it was so. This little incident had the potential to be something more than just a well-embellished story to entertain my friends with at the local watering hole for the next few months. Far more.

With everything working well enough, I decided my blood pressure had dropped to an acceptable level and it was now time to survey the damage rendered to my long-time faithful Old Red.

I pulled the door handle and heard the hinges creak like some trapdoor scene in a B-grade horror flick. The door stopped at about half its full range.

"Crap," I muttered.

Always something.

I sighed, retrieved my black leather, fur-lined gloves from the floor and began the ordeal of squeezing my one-hundred-ninety-pound frame through the opening. I keep myself in fairly good shape so it wasn't going to be too daunting of a task. Don't get me wrong, at thirty-six, I had no offers to model naked, (well, there was that one incident at the office Christmas party a couple of years back. I refused on the grounds that the security cameras were still very much functional), but I could still get around a softball field pretty well.

As I exited the car, the snow still fell, swirling gently, not as intently as a few minutes prior. I glanced around and observed slow-moving headlights gleaming from both directions, and for a moment, those lights caught the splendor of huge, dancing flakes reflecting against the evening's darkened sky. Dazzling.

Interesting the beauty one can observe in even the most stressful of situations. Then again, my stress was over. I'd made it. No worries. Be happy.

Tiptoeing with ice-induced caution toward the front of the vehicle, I could see that the hood, bumper, and engine were tangled and somewhat resembled an accordion. It was a minor miracle the door opened at all.

Perchance it would have been better, for me, if it hadn't. I guess, from my point of view, the jury is still out on that one.

Growing up, cursing in my house had been a no-no. I didn't care at that moment. I cursed. Well, mayhap. Does "Oh, horseballs!" qualify as cursing? My deceased mom, bless her heart, had infused into her three children the principle of "if you can't say something nice, shut up," so growing up there weren't many idle words floating around the Stark homestead. But given my current state of affairs, I felt reasonably sure even she would not mind the slip-up. I know that because I'd heard her say the same thing when my father came home with two new Lab puppies one Christmas. She'd said something to him about not getting close to her for a month. I figured out what that meant a little later in life.

I'm fairly new to the whole cell phone culture, so it took a moment for me to realize I didn't need to flag down a vehicle; instead I could just pull the little flip toy (I had a sweet one that reminded me of an original Star Trek communicator) out of my coat pocket and call 911.

I reached in, pulled out the black and silver phone, and flipped it open with Kirk-like flair. I saw it bounce around in my gloved fingers and promptly drop into ten inches of cold, wet snow. I didn't have Abbey Manis's flair or talent for double cursing. I gave it a shot anyway.

Twisting in the general direction the phone had done a three-and-one-half gainer, I spotted the muted blue light just beneath the bank of white.

Realizing I could still get home for hot chocolate and some trumped-up explanation to Kara that I need special treatment tonight, I bent to retrieve the accursed thing, as any reasonable person would.

That was my second mistake.

As I rummaged through the snow, I swiftly realized that my world was becoming ever so much brighter. Like football field floodlights all being switched on simultaneously.

I stood straight up and began to turn toward the perceived source of that light. Before I completed that turn, the night was shattered by the heart-stopping bellow of dual air horns speaking to my ears from a location entirely too close to exist as a good thing.

By reflex, I cupped my ears and turned just in time to see the jackknifed semi-tractor skidding directly toward me, the bright red cab looking for all of the world like blood.

There was simply no time to move or even scream, and oddly, no time to see my life flash before me for a second time in ten minutes. Not even sufficient time for an attempt at a triple curse as I watched helplessly while fifty-thousand pounds of steel and glass slammed into me. The impact drove me into Old Red with as much resistance as a ten-ounce rag doll and with all of the authority the runaway vehicle could muster. I felt everything, and then nothing.

As I think back, just before my world succumbed to the dark, I wondered how Kara and Apollo would take this.

Then I was over.

3-CHAPTER

Wonder among wonders.

The kiss from that semi-truck didn't escort me to the great mystery beyond this life, certainly not in the traditional sense, at least. To use a boxing metaphor, I was down but not out, a coma's bastard child, if you will.

During the time I journeyed through the enclaves of that coma, I dreamed dreams that ripened into something entirely different. Those dreams were eventually forced to amuse themselves because I couldn't remember them. In fact, I really didn't recall much of anything during that extraordinary expedition into the unknown, at least in the beginning.

There weren't any crystallized images of grandiose disclosure that would sufficiently guide, or conversely shame, the human race into mending its terrible ways, holding hands and singing "Kumbaya" while roasting marshmallows for s'more consumption. I love s'mores, by the way.

There was no scientific revelation regarding the human genome, or the supernatural genome, for that matter, that would give geneticists the location of the elusive "stupid" gene and the subsequent knowledge of how to eliminate it from the general population's gene pool.

I didn't even get insight on how to write the next great country song that would change the music industry forever. That would have been, well, just flat-out cool.

My rattled brain didn't foster much thought or complex recollection at all.

Other than my one utterance as I awoke.

"Your choice will impact everything, but either way, I love you."

Even now, my spine chills as I recall those words. Never has a sentence haunted, encouraged, and terrified me like that one. Of course, timing is everything in most situations, and this one is no exception. I had no idea what these words meant, or their origin, until the time came for the meaning to be revealed. That revelation would prove to be a real pisser.

Anyway, in the early morning after I became a hood ornament—three twelve a.m., to be exact— light began to penetrate my eyelids and my first reaction was one of pain. Kidney stone-like pain on steroids, as pointed as any alarm clock.

This illumination of light, herding me back to consciousness, inflicted a surprising level of agony. My eyes were hot coals. Twelve days in the dark can cause obvious sensitivity, yet I knew it was more than that.

It's interesting how the light and the dark are really not as much opposites as they might seem. They have much in common. Too much of either can cause terrifying blindness. Not enough of each, in the right circumstances, can cause untold difficulties, ranging from sleep deprivation to depression and horrendous anxiety and fear.

Our need for both the light and the dark is encrypted somewhere deep in our DNA, and I suspect, like most things in life (except vegetables and doughnuts), a balance between the two is the healthiest position to maintain.

Having said that, it's important to note since the accident, the varying degrees of light and darkness have come to mean much more to me than previously, much more than I could have imagined. And not just in the physical sense.

Slowly, with extreme trepidation, I opened and closed my eyes until finally I began to recognize substantive objects instead of dancing blurs. I saw the small television perched high on the far wall, some CNN reporter rambling about something. Whatever it was, she seemed passionate about it. That, or she was a heck of an actress.

The volume must have been down because I couldn't hear her rant. More proof that blessings come in many forms.

I continued blinking my eyes like I had sand in them. Sweet focus wasn't coming as I expected— the reporter had a sort of blue luminosity outlining her head and torso. Like a victim's chalk outline at a murder scene.

I struggled with her and the screen, finally giving in to the realization that she was going to be blue and fuzzy for a spell longer. I had other fish to fry.

Guiding my eyes away from the boob tube, I focused my attention down the pale wall of the room and stopped at two empty teal colored plastic chairs. Nothing special there, except I love that color because it reminds me of the first time I saw the Caribbean Ocean.

Oh, and for the record, the blue aura vanished once I stopped looking at the TV screen.

Both situations, thoughts of the Caribbean and the blue aura leaving my sight line, allowed a small grain of hope to filter through.

After one more reassuring glance at the teal chairs, I worked my sights to the foot of the bed, my ever-strengthening gaze stopping at the pale comforter near the steel bed frame.

White is not my favorite color, unless we're talking lingerie, but I could actually make out the small woven patterns in the blanket stretched neatly to the very tip of the bed. More hope. I began to breathe a bit easier.

Catching the television's light out of my peripheral, I instinctively glanced in that direction. The reporter was still grandstanding . . . and she was still outlined in glowing blue. I squinted and let my eyes slowly wander around her frame. The aura pulsed in almost perfect rhythm to her gestures and movements. Mesmerizing stuff because it was, well . . . shiny. Men love shiny, and I'm no exception.

That aura was magnificent. But I chalked it up to the poor quality of the TV. I watched a moment longer and then reluctantly moved on. My eyes progressed up the bed's left side. Up to that point, I didn't remember moving my head. Just my eyes. So, I tilted my chin downward to give it a try and felt a great rush of throbbing hurt come and go, twice. I was thankful the pain subsided fairly quickly because I saw immediately that I had more news to soak in.

I stared in utter amazement at the wires and tubes running under the white comforter. In the first of many epiphanies to come, I, Gabe Stark, collector extraordinaire and hot husband, realized that they were, in various ways, attached to me.

I'm in a hospital, I thought.

No shit, Sherlock, I thought again.

Let it not be said of me that I'm slow on the uptake.

This wasn't like the time Kara had slinked into the living room, as I intently watched my beloved Detroit Tigers put an old-fashioned thrashing on the hated Chicago White Sox, dressed in a short black negligee and gartered stockings.

"Nice outfit," I had said, barely turning from the game.

"Thanks."

"Why are you wearing it?"

"I thought I'd go down to the bar and see if anyone will buy me a drink."

"Better wear a jacket. You should get a bunch of takers with that get-up—ohhhhh—so, ah, should I turn off the game?"

"Depends on which score you're more interested in."

Although baseball was a close second—embarrassingly close, truth be told—there is nothing hotter than an already beautiful wife in a blistering outfit. As I said, I do eventually get the picture.

My room awareness was growing as the sounds of monitors beeping softly in the background set the rest of the hook. Then, using the infamous *out-of-nowhere* idiom, stark memories of the truck rushing toward me brought clear waves of recollection, far more than I really wanted to see. But we don't always get what we want, do we? The memories pressed harder.

I should have been dead. I should have been torn into bloody pieces like some sorry bit character victimized in a Stephen King novel, being fitted for a casket at this very moment. A very small casket, I might add.

Since the necessity of hospitals in the afterlife seemed a bit counterintuitive, I deduced that hadn't been the case and I'd survived the accident. But how could anyone endure that kind of meeting of man and machine? The answer was unmistakable; no one could. Yet, here I was. That detail was further confirmed by the encompassing antiseptic smell that accompanies all hotels of healing. My somewhat prolific nose was functioning perfectly, confirming life one final time, and I found myself damn happy about it.

I began to speak a praise to the universe, God, Odin, or whomever, but was suddenly aware of how dry my mouth and throat were.

Turning my head to the right, I sought relief. Although there was substantially more pain than when I'd tilted my chin, my head indeed moved and the pain subsided as before. It was eerie how the sharpness of the initial movement then transformed into almost no pangs of suffering at all.

The first object I saw held certain promise.

The white Styrofoam cup on the brown tray, with its sassy red and white bent straw pointing high, seemed innocent . . . at first. But looks can be deceiving. I gave it my best Clint Eastwood stare.

The little hussy must have known how parched I was. The small, beads of condensation winked in the light, mocking me, daring me to get some of its juice or water or whatever it held. She knew what I wanted. I swear I heard her say, "*In your dreams, Big Boy.*"

I've been denied my way a few times in my life, especially in my given profession, but this little heifer wasn't going to be the next installment on that long list.

I raised my hand toward it. Again, there was pain, but the arm moved, and then the pain disappeared. Evidently I hadn't broken *every* bone in my body.

My hand stretched closer, and I smiled inwardly. *In my dreams, huh?*

Closer yet, and I was almost giddy. My hand was shaky but still moving. Soon that little wench would eat her words.

Five inches from the cup, my hand stopped thanks to a bundle of wires and tubes. Exceedingly disappointed, I found I lacked the strength to keep reaching for my goal. I dropped my hand to the comforter, defeated.

The cup grinned. *"I told you, dumbass,"* she mocked.

"I'll get you."

"Not in this life, Bedsore Boy."

"You're pissing me off."

"So?"

I swear she laughed.

"Paybacks are hell, white trash," I whispered, not taking my eyes from the cup.

"Yep, they are. But you won't be getting any."

"Get a grip, Gabe. It's a cup," I said to myself.

"You won't be doing that for a while either," she said, grinning.

I turned my head away from the vixen, contemplating my next step. I felt like a pawn in the *Game of Thrones*.

As far as I can remember, that was my first level of frustration toward my condition. I had no idea what was accomplished by surviving the truck's ferocious smooch, only to die of thirst in that bed. Particularly brutal when one considered that the evil Styrofoam cup was my would-be assassin.

With a little more effort, I refocused and got rid of the pity party. *Hey, I am alive,* I reminded myself again. And I know hospitals. The nurse would be in soon. After all, it was her job, right? Then I could have a heart-to-heart with the cup. Just her and me. One on one.

I closed my eyelids, thinking perhaps a little rest would help me regain some strength and sanity to boot. The cup's ass was mine. I just had to be patient. I can do patient.

Not long after I closed my eyes, I felt it. The hot stare boring a hole in my face had to be Kara. Who else? Elation carried me into the stratosphere even before I moved my eyelids. I couldn't wait to see her.

But I would have to. When I opened my eyes, my beloved wife wasn't sitting in the chair on the left, but instead, a total stranger.

He sat with legs crossed in such a way so as not to crease the trousers of his obviously tailored white tuxedo, complete with cummerbund and gloves. Neither of us spoke as we sized each other up.

The most obvious attribute belonging to my visitor was his eyes. They were large and the color of lilac lavender. Contacts, I guessed.

Spooky nonetheless.

This well-dressed man was of average height and build and really only possessed average looks, except those inescapable eyes that held my attention as if I had absolutely no choice in the matter.

Unfolding his legs, he stood with the grace of a highly skilled dancer, and consequently broke the spell of his astonishing stare. That's when I noticed something else. His eyes weren't his only unique attribute.

The golden-hilted sword hung at his hip. It clung to his side like a loyal sidekick and seemed to move with him like it had life of its own. I shifted my uneasy gawk back to his face and got the immediate impression that I wasn't the only anxious one in the room.

This sword-carrying reject from a sixties wedding party . . . what could he possibly be nervous about? From my disadvantaged point of view, he was holding all of the cards and a big-ass sword to boot.

"Who are you?" My whispered inquiry sounded like I had spent the night singing karaoke in a smoky bar.

The pale clad visitor shifted weight to his left foot, looked to the floor, and then to the ceiling.

"You can see me, then?"

It was my turn to survey the room. I wondered how I had been so fortunate as to draw a visitor with invisible-man psychosis. Could I be in the psych ward? Kara had warned me it could happen if I didn't straighten out my act.

The hits just kept right on a'coming.

"Ahh . . . yes, I can see you," I croaked. "Is that a problem?"

With blinding speed, his glower never leaving me, he whirled around the foot of the bed, heading straight toward me, his white-gloved hand clutching the weapon at his side.

This unusual, simple looking but terrifying man bent to within an inch of my face wearing the faint beginnings of a wry smile.

"I expected someone different than you, *much* different," he whispered.

Then he was gone, vanishing into a curl of iridescent vapor.

4-CHAPTER

In what was surely an optical illusion born to confuse me more, a woman, who I knew as Nurse Peggy Charles, seemed to appear at the foot of my bed as quickly as the mysterious stranger had departed. It was as if his vaporization had created a hole in the fabric of space and time through some confusing law of physics or entropy or Humpty Dumpty or something else unknown to me. I don't get all of that scientific stuff, so I was taken aback, briefly, that those thoughts had entered my mind at all. (Well, I do get the Humpty Dumpty reference, sort of. Come on. Putting an egg back together after it drops from a high wall? Really?)

Perhaps a tad melodramatic, but that is how I perceived this substitute of character, so to speak. As if that little replacement trick hadn't been enough, there was something else about my caretaker. The same type of aura I had noticed around the TV reporter engulfed Nurse Peggy. It was lighter in color, but there wasn't any question regarding the pattern around her physical being. Odd I hadn't remembered that about the sword man.

I blinked a couple of times, but the fascinating aura remained. I told myself again that my visual focus would come around, give it some time, what did I expect? I had been a thin hair away from evolving into frozen road kill, so some things aren't going to work so well right away, if ever. I didn't like the sound of that in my head, reality or not.

Refocusing on Peggy Charles, I offered some weak attempt at smiling. That hurt too, but the pain left quickly enough. I was sensing a pattern here.

If moving my face muscles hurt in such a manner, I briefly wondered what it was going to be like when I had to pee. I shivered, deciding to go there only when absolutely necessary, like when the whites of my eyes were indeed pee-yellow.

"Hey, Gabe," she said in that soft, sultry voice that hadn't changed over the years.

"Hey, Peggy," I rasped.

My nurse and I were well met, as they say. In fact, I had dated her in high school.

After a few rendezvous, each accompanied by her father *and* mother *and* her younger brother who played the role of a chastity belt, we decided that this wasn't the romantic path written in the stars for either of us . . . or maybe her father had made that decision. Either way, my first love and I split with only a few kisses to brag about.

We had, however, remained friends over the years. She possessed the dark complexion authored from Italian descent and her tall, model-like frame hadn't changed five pounds from our school days. Her dark eyes completed a truly beautiful woman.

She did eventually marry and mothered three children, in spite of the horrifying rigors of double-dating with one's parents until the age of eighteen.

Another, more pragmatic, side to her was Peggy's refreshingly candid take on life. I knew she would answer my questions with her fabled honesty. This nurse boasted the unique bedside manner that enabled her to put the knife through your ribs as you begged for more. She completely embodied the old saying that it is really not what one says, but how it's said.

Our eyes met, and I saw unexpected astonishment, joy, and another less discernable emotion.

"Good to see you awake, handsome," she soothed.

I told you she was unequivocally truthful.

"We weren't sure when we would get to see those blue eyes again," she added.

I looked at her as the words began to register, but in that moment, it occurred to me that I was extremely groggy. Odd. I hadn't felt that way when the man in the white get-up had visited. Seconds passed for my response time to work. It was like being in a time-delayed broadcast of one of those damned NFL games in London.

"I'm . . . I'm . . . hey, I do have blue eyes, don't I?"

Pretty clever, I thought.

"Yes, you do. I see the pain medication is still working."

Another lag. "You're the doctor. How come my hair hurts?"

Her turn to smile. "I think I can fix that, and I'm the nurse, remember?"

Less lag. "Okay. I knew that. Can I get up?"

She started toward me then hesitated, which wasn't really like the Peggy Charles I'd known. She cast her eyes downward, as if she required some wisdom from the medical chart hanging at the end of the bed.

The glow surrounding her turned a notch brighter, then subsided quickly. Kind of like an oncoming auto whose driver failed to switch headlights from bright to dim. I could see what I thought were tears silently materializing over her large eyes. But being the professional she was, they were only momentary visitors.

"We'll see what the doctors have to say about that one, Gabe. Can I do anything else?"

I did my best to motion toward the demon cup to my right, but she was far ahead of me and already around the bed holding the cup of ice-cold water to my desert-dry lips.

The first couple of swallows hurt, as if my throat had been scored by a feisty feline, but then it was me and the cup, just like old times, except I was getting my revenge. She had met with her reckoning, and it was me. I found myself hoping the little slut would be recycled and it would hurt so very much.

I won, just as I predicted.

"Easy there, big boy. Too much too soon won't be a good thing for you or me. I'll have to clean up the mess," Peggy said.

Finally understanding her point, I snorted and then laughed, cold water gushing from my right nostril. Not my favorite memory from that early morning.

My body convulsed and suddenly felt like it had been walloped with the truck all over again. Everything hurt like I'd been beaten with hammers, and not those tiny jeweler rigs either. Then it didn't.

"Sorry," she said, cringing. "Laughing, coughing, and sneezing are going to hurt for a few days at least."

"Duly noted," I answered a few seconds later without telling her I didn't feel any pain now. I'd wait on that one.

"Also, I'm sure you are feeling a little groggy. The delay in your cognitive functions isn't you, it's the pain medicine."

Focusing on her face, I did my best to catch up in real time. It was coming along, but the glow around her head was becoming an issue. It almost hurt my eyes.

I closed my peepers and concentrated on getting them to concentrate only on her physical embodiment.

When I opened them, the blue-white annoyance had virtually dissipated. My eyes *were* getting better, as I'd suspected.

One battle down, for now, but there was another issue I needed to discuss.

The white-clad visitor.

I wasn't totally sure about what I was contemplating, but he seemed as genuinely real as Peggy, and if he had been here, she would have seen him exit the room. That supposition made sense to me; even in the drug-induced state I was semi-enjoying. Okay. *Really* enjoying.

She hadn't mentioned him, however, or acknowledged that he'd been at the foot of my bed just moments ago.

I had little choice regarding the next vein of conversation between us. I was compelled and frankly had no real desire to curb that compulsion. I had to ask. She might say it was the drugs, which could have been true, I suppose. But even then, I knew in my heart of hearts, that he'd been there.

I inhaled as much air as my on again, off again, pain-racked body would allow and thought about a clever way to bring Old Purple Eyes into the conversation.

"So was the guy in the white outfit and the golden sword a doctor?"

Peggy's smile slowly melted to nothing. "What guy? What sword?"

"You really didn't see him? He was here, leaning over me just before you entered. White tux, crazy purple eyes, *Dancing with the Stars* reject, that guy."

"Darlin', I've been the only one in your room in the last hour. My station is just outside this IC room and no one came in or out, not even Kara. She's still asleep in the guest waiting room."

Again, it took a moment, but my eyes narrowed like a bill collector who had been informed that the check was in the mail.

Peggy shook her head and took my hand. "Look, sometimes when people meander out of comas, it's like sailing from fog to bright sunshine. You were obviously dreaming. I'll bet two chocolate Santas that's what was going on with you. Besides, hospital policy requires all swords to be checked in at the security desk."

"You're a funny girl."

"Smart too," she countered.

I thought about her logical explanation, and it made absolute sense. Moreover, people just don't dissolve in front of one's eyes, not even while riding the roller-coaster of hardcore pain medicine. Although doubt still pulled me in a more intuitive direction, I had to go with the probabilities Peggy had recited.

I reluctantly moved on to a more urgent disclosure she had made.

"How long was I in the coma?" The water had made speaking a measure easier. I actually was beginning to sound like me, or at least less like a desperate frog.

By then, she'd pulled her cell phone from her pocket and was waiting for it to ring. She gave me the wait-just-a-second look as she addressed the party she'd dialed.

"You may want to come in here, now," she said then hung up.

She took my hand again. "Twelve days, Gabe. Not so long considering the . . ." she hesitated, again, "severity of your accident."

She exhaled like she'd just run up three flights of steps. It seemed like she was having more difficulty controlling her emotion with each passing second.

These out-of-character-behaviors were beginning to create a somewhat nervous condition in me.

Fear.

Being the consummate professional, Nurse Peggy must have seen something in my eyes and changed the subject.

"By the way, just before you came back from the coma world, you said, '*Your choice will impact much, but either way, I love you*'. You said it several times, in fact. Do you remember what that was about?"

I dwelled on her question for a few moments, and then made a brief and almost painless shake of the noggin. I had no idea the source of that delirium. It sounded kind of cool, however.

I motioned for another drink, noticing that the little harlot of a cup had grown silent, apparently accepting defeat. I grinned, sending the Styrofoam abomination the finger in my mind's eye.

Peggy obliged, and I drank deeply.

I then leaned back and peered at her as to demand attention. She gave it to me.

Gathering courage I didn't always possess, I asked the next hard question, maybe the most difficult.

"Peggy, you've always been straight with me so tell me just how severe was my accident?"

"I'll answer that, Gabriel."

Undeniably, there are moments in each of our lives that can, and do, help define just where we stand in the copious picture that the cosmic universe has painted, no matter how insignificant or dramatic our impact on that universe.

Hearing Kara's melodic voice at that moment was one for me.

There are no words existing in any language, human or otherwise, able to define the qualities projected in her four words.

I heard unconditional love, concern, relief, and gratitude in her expressive response. Gabe Stark's "too manly to cry" mantra had just flown out the window.

I began an effort to turn to her—a silly notion on my part. She was there in an instant, cradling my face with both hands raining kisses on me like I had just won the lotto. I suppose I had.

Her hands were soft and warm; her breathe fresh and alive. That probably had something to do with the candy cane she had used as a breath mint, but outrageously enjoyable just the same. Oh yeah, that annoying glow was back, and this time, stronger than any prior, and only around Kara.

She stepped back, grinned, and repeated the whole kissy-face thing again. Our Lab Apollo would have been proud.

"Okay, okay. I'm all right." I said with as much masculine demeanor as I could muster. That, however, didn't prevent a third molestation. Thank God.

"I'll leave you two, and see if I can rustle up the shift doctor to peek in on you . . . and no fooling around, at least until the doc leaves," said Peggy with a grin.

Kara put her hands on her hips in feigned frustration. "What? Okay. We'll wait for the doctor to hit the door."

I loved the sound of her voice. Music from heaven.

After Nurse Peggy had exited, Kara pulled up the same chair that my imaginary visitor had used and grasped my right hand. That one had only three small tubes running into it.

"When they called me, well . . . I'm so glad you're alive," she whispered, fighting tears that were asking me to match them.

I fought hard but lost.

That wasn't the extent of what was happening in good old room twelve.

The aura outlining my wife grew so intense it caused me to squint. There was no pain, just the light. Her light.

I repeated the focusing exercise, hoping to clear the aura from my vision, and surprisingly succeeded a second time, like with the nurse and reporter. My eyes seemed to be genuinely screwed up but things could have been decidedly worse.

Great. I was going to have to endure eye-transplant surgery, and the way my luck was running, I'd get new peeps from a condemned serial killer that would force me to do terrible, unthinkable things.

I know . . . too much television.

The whole lag thing with my brain was improving, so I was able to respond quicker.

"From what I can recall, and what Peggy shared, I'm not sure I should be."

"You, I'm, we are truly lucky that someone was watching out for you because the people at the scene were amazed you weren't . . . gone."

I was detecting another theme here.

Kara tilted her head. "You did, however, check out once, in the ambulance on the way to the hospital."

"I died?"

"That's what they tell us."

I pondered that wisp of information for a moment or two, and then let it go. There would be more time to contemplate such things later. As it turned out, not that much later.

I then decided to change the subject, sort of.

"So tell me, what's broken?"

Kara stared at me, glanced over my head, then back to my face.

"You broke several ribs, causing a puncture of your left lung. Your left arm has compound fractures of the radius and ulna. You snapped your left femur, cracked your pelvis, and actually fractured your skull in two places. Fourteen bones in all. You also shattered three teeth, your left ear was partially torn way, and you no longer have a spleen."

She looked to the floor and swallowed, sought composure, then continued in a quiet, and frankly, disturbing tone. "Your clothes were so tattered, and there was so much blood, they . . . they . . . they really didn't notice that your—" Tears, the big crocodile kind, welled, and this time there was no effort to squelch the saline flow.

Any mental lag I may have previously experienced was now completely obliterated. She had my full attention. I just knew she was having a difficult time relaying to me that I was now a full-blown, card-carrying eunuch.

How was I going to pee?

I exhibited my best *braver-than-any-man-who-has-ever-lived* face, swallowed hard, and asked the next sixty-four-thousand-dollar question.

"What are you trying to say, honey?"

She reached for the box of blue tissues on the meal tray, wiping away tears so intense I swore I could smell them.

Kara stood up, moved to the left side of the bed, careful to avoid the tangle of tubing and delicate wires disappearing under my comforter, and gently rolled the blanket to my waist.

"I'm so sorry, Gabe. They tried to save it, but—"

I looked down to where she was looking and saw the white cast ended just above my left knee. My lower leg was gone.

5-CHAPTER

I continued to stare, looked back to Kara, then back to where my leg customarily resided. I repeated that disbelieving routine several times. No leg? MIA?

"Speechless" and I had never been related, but at that moment we were the closest of brothers.

She sat down beside me and grasped my hand in hers again. "The surgeons finished removing it because it was shredded from the impact and hardly attached to your knee, it hung by a couple of ligaments. You, apparently, at the last second jumped to avoid the truck, but it caught your entire left side, slamming you into Old Red."

As Kara spoke, I listened without truly hearing.

When I was a child and had made a mistake, like young children (and old children for that matter) do, my father seldom struck his offspring for such indiscretions, but instead took advantage of our errors in judgment to yell at us for long periods of time.

Honestly, I often wished he would have just warmed my cheeks and gotten the whole thing over with. During those screaming and reaming episodes, my mind would simply go numb and then separate into a truly definable out-of-body experience.

Necessity is indeed the mother of invention, and I suppose my mind created this "leaving" as some type of defense mechanism to avoid the reality of the situation. We do what we must.

I now felt that old familiar departure of mind from body. Kara must have known it and stopped speaking. She gently put one hand on each side of my bruised face and kissed me.

My wife always knows how to harvest my attention. Mission accomplished.

"You saved your life by jumping, but the leg caught on the truck's horned bumper and, well, was virtually disintegrated by the impact. There wasn't enough left to repair and reattach. I'm so sorry, Gabe."

I looked away from her, back to where my leg should have been.

The questions were already bombarding me. I couldn't help it. *Why me? What did I do to deserve this? How could I ever be a complete man again? Why is this fair?*

I've done my best to live a good life. I helped orphans and gave people breaks on bills they had no money to pay. I was a Good Samaritan, more or less. Why did God, if He is really out there, let this happen to me instead of someone who deserved it, like the Taliban or Congress?

You get the picture. Furthermore, on top of my newly developed emotional anguish, my whole body was beginning to throb in painful rhythm to my heartbeat. This time, the pain stayed. Whether this was a result of my emotional despair at losing my leg or true physical discomfort, it made no significant difference to me. I was a hurting puppy and needed relief, of every kind imaginable.

I know far too well what transpires when pain and anger are made unwilling bedfellows.

I was pissed.

Even in that indescribable frustration, I reminded myself that Kara was the unwilling messenger and to not direct my growing vexation toward her. I was determined not to break my vow of never raising my voice to my wife. I learned early in life how damning that can be. Besides, that would be akin to trashing an extraordinary, exotic rose.

With all of the restraint I could muster, I spoke, impressing myself with my controlled tone.

"I'm tired and the pain is really kicking in. Could you get the nurse or the doctor? Then I think I'd like to be alone for a while."

Kara reached past my head and did something to one of the tubes running into my arm.

"That will take care of the physical pain, Gabe. And I know you've gone through a lot in the last half hour, and I'm with you. Get some rest, and I'll be here when you're ready to talk about the leg. Or anything else. I love you."

She kissed me again and walked out of the room. But not before the radiance surrounding her returned. I added the fact that my eyes were now undeniably and totally screwed up to the list of things fueling my jerk-off attitude. But the attitude was understandable, right?

Fortunately, whatever drug she released into my battered system was beginning to work its welcomed magic as the pain retreated to whatever level of hell it had come from.

At least the physical pain was subsiding.

I closed my eyes, hoping, praying that I had just experienced the most vivid nightmare of my life and I would wake again as healthy, normal, good ol' Gabe.

All a bad dream.

I allowed myself the frail, emotional luxury of the lie. Depression was knocking on the door and wanted in too. Funny how those two jokers walked down the aisle together. Well, not funny, but you know what I mean.

"Bastards," I whispered.

"So, how's you feelin', mon?"

With more effort than anticipated, I opened my eyes to see my third, maybe fourth if you count the white-clad man, visitor.

The ebony face seemed to be all teeth, with gold wire rims floating just above them. She had dark dreadlocks, streaked with auburn red, and I had serious doubt if anyone in North Haven was thinner. She bore a striking resemblance to Cleopatra's unwrapped mummy. Oddly enough, it wasn't until later, much later, that I would realize this good doctor possessed no aura about her, at least none that I could see.

"Who are you? Never mind, I don't give a dog's fart, just get out."

"Whoa, a wee bit touchy, I see. Well dat's understandable, given recent developments I s'pose. I'm Doctor Nadia Thomas."

"Great, I'm happy for you, now get out. Go eat eight or nine pizzas."

"We can't bond if we don't talk, don't you tink?"

"I'm tired, I lost a leg, I hurt, and you're pissing me off. How's that for meaningful, bonding conversation?"

"Better den my first husband, for sure."

I grinned, even though I fought the urge like a crying child who finds something funny and disrupts his surly mood.

"You were married?"

"Yeah, I'm really quite sexy when I put on tirty pounds. I'm skinny like dis to keep da man-folk off me."

She had me. I liked Dr. Nadia Thomas already, but I didn't want her to know. I just wanted to wallow in self-pity, and self-pity is a jealous heifer. I turned away and didn't answer.

Dr. Thomas moved closer, standing three feet from my bed. "I saw dat grin, mon. You be feelin' it for my skinny ass, don't ya?"

"What? Feeling it for you? Whatever. You're delusional."

"Yep. People, day say dat about me before, ya know?"

She swung around to the other side of the bed.

"You be one lucky white boy. Someone, they be a'watchin' out for you. I jus' want ya ta know, ya are surely going ta make a full recovery from dat tangle wit de truck. I want ta help anyway I can along da way. I can answer most all da questions running around in dat brain. If you wanna talk to me, I be a good listener, ya know?"

I finally had enough. Remember what my mom used to say about saying things? Well, that went by the wayside, along with my lower leg.

"How would you know what's going on with me?" I seethed. "You doctors are great at saying you get it, but how in the hell could you? You have no damn idea what's going through my mind."

She gazed at me for a time, like she was wrestling with a decision that would rock civilization to its collective knees.

Slowly, she removed the loose-fitting blue smock and matching synthetic gloves, exposing one bare arm . . . and one constructed of a white synthetic substance blended with silver metal alloy. The fingers of the prosthesis had colored wires running to the wrist and looked like something out of a futuristic cyborg flick, which I'm totally addicted to.

I was horrified and fascinated at the same time.

She apparently saw that, and so continued.

"Dis new arm is compliments of a twelve-foot black tip shark at home in Dominica."

"Really?"

"I shit ya not, Gabriel Stark. When I was fourteen, I jus' be swimming along wit my friends in da beautiful Caribbean Ocean, like we do back home, and dis big boy tought I be lunch for him. He got it almost right, ya know? But I lived, and da rest be history. So as you can see, I do have an idea what's going on wit ya."

I had felt a plethora of emotions that morning, but the shame I felt now was new. She had nearly experienced what many experts call the worst fear that human's harbor—to be eaten alive.

At that moment, I barely remembered why I was in the hospital. I had such compassion for the tiny teenager who was Doctor Thomas those years ago and wasn't even sure why I was feeling that deeply, but I was.

It was as if I had crawled into her very body and soul. I felt what she had felt the moment the shark had clamped onto her, rolling its dark, lifeless eyes, ripping off her thin arm the very next instant.

I swear I could smell the saltwater, feel the hot sun, and literally taste her unbridled terror. Unsettling was not a strong enough word. Damn Freaky?

All I know is that my anxiety over my accident paled in comparison to the emotion of her attack.

I hate lessons like this. Even when it's for my own edification.

I don't know. Maybe it was the meds bringing a heightened sense of empathy, or maybe I was already beginning to accept what had happened. Regardless, I let the tears loose, realizing the saying was true: there is always someone worse off than you.

She grinned, as she replaced her coat. "I love to see men cry, ya know?"

"Yeah, well you still need to eat a few hundred burgers."

I know, but it was my best comeback.

Her toothy expression turned more serious. "If a scared little girl from dat poor little island country can make it witout da love and support you have, well den, you got no worries, ya?"

I gave her my best nod of understanding. She had trumped my ace, and the rest of my cards didn't seem so playable either.

"I'll be here for you when you want ta talk. I promise."

Then Dr. Nadia Thomas performed the most unorthodox, unexpected, and simultaneously incredible thing any doctor could do. She kissed my forehead, sealing her promise to me. That act isn't in any medical textbook, I guessed. But it made me feel better, and after all, that is the name of the game. I appreciated her tenderness in more ways than she could imagine.

After she left, I felt worn to the proverbial frazzle, allowing sleep to come much easier. I indulged. I don't know for sure how long I was out, but I awoke abruptly to another unexpected surprise.

Did I mention that the hits just kept coming?

My violet-eyed friend in the white tux had returned.

6-CHAPTER

My first inclination was to tie his peculiar existence with the introduction of the ever-present abundance of pain medication, but even after I closed and opened my eyes several times, he remained. I had to give him credit for being a persistent little hallucination. Along with that, I was developing a much better understanding of the term "overstaying one's welcome."

"So, you're not a dream or a drug-induced phantasm?"

He shook his head, slowly, his eyes alive. "No, Gabriel, hardly."

He gave me the tiny beginning of a sardonic smile and introduced himself. "My name is Samuel; please do not refer to me as Sam. I'm not a creation of Doctor Seuss or any other such silliness."

I frowned. "How do you know my name?"

"I know many things . . . and much about you,
I might add."

His response did little to settle the
matriculating butterflies that had begun
synchronized tumbling drills within the confines of
my stomach.

"Great," I muttered. "You're a stalker then?"

"I believe your phrase was meant to be a
measured word of sarcasm, but it contains truth,
Gabriel."

"It was just a term. Sorry you were offended.
Wait. I actually don't care if you were."

"Even at that last statement, I wasn't. I've seen
far too much to be affronted by misguided words."
He then stepped to my side again, touching my
arm.

His hand was cool to the touch, but there was
an unacknowledged power in that contact.

That wasn't all. This . . . this *being*, Samuel,
gazed at . . ., no, scoped me out, with the intensity
of a woman who just found lipstick on her
husband's collar.

I don't know how I knew, but he seemed to be
filing more details about me in his mind, much
like a digital camera taking pictures of a particular
subject from every angle—except this was deeper,
like some kind of sophisticated x-ray analysis that
would tell him how fractured and susceptible I

might be to any one of an inventory of mental or physical conditions or diseases.

In short, was I as broken on the inside as the out?

I could have answered him far more conventionally if he would have asked.

I was pretty sure I was going freaking crazy and couldn't halt that rodeo.

Waiting another moment, he then asked the oddest question, thinking it was rather anomalous at the time.

"Gabriel. Do you believe this world to be evil or good?"

My mind was going through that little time-delay thing again, but his presence seemed to somehow make that better, clearer. I thought about his question, forgetting my lost leg as I pondered that angle of humanity. I usually took things on the surface and simply figured people had junk to deal with. The concept of evil intent was a little over the top for me.

"I guess we have our problems, but I think people are basically good, so I would have to say good. I do, however, think diseases, like cancer, and events, such as famines, earthquakes, floods, etcetera, are not good things."

I looked at him, my new condition waltzing fresh through my mind. "You can throw maiming into that mix."

I was on a soapbox now.

"And abundant disregard for life leading to murder. And child abuse. People, including children, seem to be disrespectful, and why in the name of God can't young men pull up their pants and stop grabbing their crotches? Also, why does every spring line of women's clothing have—"

I stopped. My mouth was quickly constructing a statement contrary to my answer to Samuel's peculiar, but purposeful query. Maybe this third rock from the sun wasn't in such virtuous condition after all.

His eyes grew brighter. Then he responded as if he were reading my mind, what was left of it.

"Your response is as expected. Perhaps a bit more positive than I would have assumed."

Samuel hesitated, seeming to gather thoughts that far exceeded my own.

I didn't *know* but *felt* it was true.

This intuition thing was getting kind of cool.

"Your world, humanity's world, as it were, has been near the center of an unseen, relentless siege from the very beginning of your creation here. Horrendously evil forces trying to impose their will against all that is true and good. While choices are still yours—human choices, I mean—to make, evil has tremendous influence in your seemingly coming demise."

A little melodramatic for me was an understatement. Demise of human kind? We're messed up but . . . seriously, demise?

I wanted to roll my eyes and turn up the medicinal flow.

I, however, didn't reach for the nurse's button, and I found myself wondering why. Not to mention, I really wasn't in a position to leave the room and call for the guys in the clean white coats. *Coming to take me away . . . ho-ho, hee-hee, ha-ha . . .*

I returned his stare and then looked away.

The real kicker here was that unfortunately he had my inner attention because deep down, I sensed a bizarre, frightening truth locked away in his outlandish statement.

Sidestepping what human destruction might mean to a man frolicking in the recesses of wonderful pain medicine, I went in a different direction with my next question.

Let's find out who is truly crazy here.

"What do you mean, 'your world'?" I asked.

"It is not mine. I dwell elsewhere. It was not created for the likes of me, and I don't originate from this earth."

Okay. That cleared things up for me as to which one of us was truly bongo nutsy. I felt like I was watching some kind of fantasy flick just released from Joss Wheaton's incredible imagination. I had enough on my plate without this junk rising up and robbing me of some really good pity-party time.

This was getting out of hand.

I began searching for the emergency button. Samuel squeezed my arm gently.

I stopped. The man had a charisma, there was no doubting that.

"You asked, and Gabriel, I never lie."

"Never?"

"Never."

"Okay. If you're not from earth, then where?"

"You're not ready for that."

"Why not?"

"You wouldn't be able to comprehend what I said to you. It would be like trying to explain red. I'd have to show you, and I dare say, at least for now, that would drive you insane."

I snorted. I had news for him. He wasn't the only one teetering on the abyss of a virtually certifiable nut case. He had company.

But insane was probably too easy of a deduction so I glanced around the room, looking for the film crew of *Candid Camera.*

Reading my mind again, Samuel said, "This is no joke, Gabriel."

I exploded. "Then why in hell are you here? I've been out of it for twelve days, I lost my freaking leg, and my body is so banged up that it will take months to get out of here. That means I'll have bedsores the size of baseballs, and let's not mention learning to walk with some metal contraption strapped to my knee that would scare even the Count de Sade. I'll never move normally again. On top of all that, my eyes are broken."

"Gabriel."

"What?"

The mystic quality in his voice cut to the center of my being and brought me back to him. It was as if I'd heard him with my soul and not my ears.

"Your eyes are not broken. You have gained a gift, an insight that will serve you and many others well, if used properly."

He moved closer to the bed without looking away.

"The aura you see around others reflects their state of being, their essences, if you will. You are now able to see, and sometimes feel, that state of being. When I asked if the world is good or evil, you said you thought most people were good. That is true. But there are others, influenced by and enticed into the darkest of evils. This evil only exists to cause chaos and destroy what is good, including those who embrace that virtue."

He drew ever closer, his eyes pulsating.

I felt my mouth go dry as my veins became as icy as the December weather stalking outside my window.

"You, as a seer, have the ability to perceive the condition and intentions of the human heart. You may have already experienced the intensity of that focus."

My head swam as Samuel's words slashed through my perception of reality.

Good versus evil? Demise? Golden sword? A seer? It sounded like an excerpt from one of Stan Lee's newest comic books.

As my thoughts turned toward what I'd seen— the spike in Peggy's aura and how Kara caused my eyes to hurt with her "glow"—my mind dug deeper. *How am I in some way able to control what I see around those women? What about the quick reduction of pain when I begin to hurt? Good God, why am I even alive?*

The physical laws I held as earthly strongholds were starting to crumble like a condemned building during demolition. Furthermore, how could Samuel know about what I had seen? I had said nothing to any of my visitors.

Never one to beat around the axiomatic bush, as my profession might indicate, I deemed it time to spring the obvious questions.

"Why me?"

He expressed no discernable surprise or concern, as I expected.

"You chose this course."

"What? When? It's not like picking from a lunch menu, you know. I think I would remember if I *chose* such a thing."

That crap-eating grin again. "You will remember. It will all come back to you in due time, when you're ready."

I had run out of things to say, and his cryptic answers increased the pain in my head. Was I just supposed to take all of this to heart on a man's, or whatever he was, word? I didn't know the answer to that.

By now, Samuel stood mere inches from me.

"There is one, near you, planning to perpetrate a great wrong, a treacherous act that will change North Haven's fate forever. Many will die. If accomplished, it will be a great battle won for those who would destroy the life on this planet."

"So stop him or whatever. Why don't you do it? Why don't you stop this . . . this act?" I asked with more than a hint of desperate dread.

"I am but a messenger. I told you, I don't belong here. The battle is yours."

"Messenger? Who sent you? From where?"

He ignored my query and backed away, slowly placing his pale hand on his sword, which was no longer golden, but now glowing deep crimson and pulsing with heartbeat-like rhythms. He cocked his head slightly and seemed to be listening to a silent sonata performed for only him.

Suddenly, with that same unbelievable speed, he grabbed my hand and spoke with unnerving urgency.

"Gabriel, you haven't much time, perhaps mere days, before this event of destruction is to play out. There is another who can provide direction. You must find that help if you are to succeed."

My head hurt even more. Days? I would be confined to a hospital bed for at least two months, I surmised. This was all becoming too much for me to get my mind around. It had to be a dream. Incredibly vivid, true, but a dream nonetheless.

Even if I believed everything Samuel spoke to be real, to be the truth—which I didn't—how would I ever do what he suggested? Where would I start? How do I find the "other" who can help? The local authorities might have a problem with a one-legged madman knocking on doors, asking to see glowing auras of every inhabitant of the house.

Hello, miss. Don't worry, I'm on a mission to save this planet. I'm not crazy, I'd simply like to see you aura, okay? You may stay dressed, of course.

They would fit me for a little white jacket, for sure, and take me to a place that administered SERIOUS meds to its occupants.

I needed some chocolate. Like a truckload.

Glancing around the room, I prayed my manifestation born from physical trauma would be a distant memory when I returned to the spot where he had stood. No such luck. Still there.

He stood as motionless as a marble statue. My new acquaintance was as persistent as my mother-in-law's nagging.

I tried reason. "Samuel. I'm in this bed with twelve broken bones and no lower left leg. Even if I have this seer thing, there is nothing I can do about it. Maybe we should just call the sheriff's office and warn them—."

His gaze, brighter than ever, forced me to stop in midsentence.

"It has to be you. You are the only one. Find the other who can help, the one who holds a secret."

Samuel looked to the ceiling, wrestling with a contemplation I didn't get. Whatever transpired in those thoughts, he made up his mind quickly.

"As I said, time is not a luxury we possess. There is one thing I can do. Do you believe you will heal?"

Another odd question, but I recalled what Dr. Thomas had said. I figured I could be tough, sometimes. I wasn't sure how a severed-leg wound healed. Did it truly matter? I wasn't going to give up.

"Yes, eventually."

Nodding, looking not at the ceiling but through it, I believed, he whispered something and bowed slightly.

With that, he drew the weapon resting at his side and raised it above his head. Before I could object, he pivoted a three-sixty on his heel, like some Quickening scene from a *Highlander* movie, and brought the glowing sword down across my midsection. I recall a faint odor of burning sulfur as the blade danced through the still air, as if the sword had moved with sufficient speed to create white-hot flames.

The pain was beyond intense, and the mote of stars arrayed in incredible color and intensity filled my vision momentarily.

Then darkness descended upon me like a New York blackout.

7-CHAPTER

I came to, resting in a state of clarity—for the first time in six hours.

I didn't fully understand what Samuel had done to me, but any thoughts I had of dreams and hallucinations were now in the past. Whatever was going on, I had to choose it as reality simply because it was all that I could see. I hear it's not good to mix pain medication with strong drink, but I was praying for one of those strong shots of Irish whisky anyway.

I was no longer in that hospital bed wired to gadgets and drip bags. The snow around my feet made that perfectly clear. I certainly wasn't in Kansas anymore, so to speak.

Looking up, I saw the old Victorian house looming in front of me, one that I'd remembered visiting as a kid, confirming everything I'd just run through my mind.

I squinted at the house and was hit with a rapid succession of memories.

On Halloween night as a kid, as was the custom of most small towns, we'd not only enact the expected and pleasant trick-or-treat ritual—without the destruction of property that has grown popular over the years—but also indulged in our own version of a haunted house dare. This grand old structure had been the object of that dare.

Each year, we held the omnipresent contest to see who could get the closest, and God forbid, even knock on the door. Only the most courageous among us awaited the opening of that door by one of our gang.

I did it once.

As the door had drawn slowly open, seemingly on its own, obligatory creaking and all, I'd suddenly felt my bladder loosen and then sprinted for the nearby underbrush, thankful no one could see the small stain spreading over the crotch of my homemade hobo outfit in the dark.

And before you judge me too harshly; I challenge you to the same unholy action this next Halloween.

Uh-huh. That's what I thought.

At any rate, the champion haunted-house brave heart among us got to choose one item from everyone else's bag of goodies. There was nothing like spoils to the victor.

There would be no such champion now.

I didn't know what time it was, I only know that it was dark—pitch black, to be precise—and cold. Yet the consistency of the dark seemed different. I think I could have reached out and scooped some of it with my hand and put it in my pocket. I was not inclined to test that theory for fear that I'd be right. Not to mention, I wasn't sure I had pockets.

That darkness was interrupted by two separate sources of light. One soft glow of flickering illumination frittered and danced through the three-by-three window near the wide front door, allowing me to see the entrance. An educated guess said that light originated from a rather substantial fireplace.

The other light came from the foremost of the four oblong, tapered gables marking the corners of the house above me. That light was different. It seemed the complete antithesis of the dark surrounding this grand building. It glowed steadily with a sort of unnatural strength that held an undefined draw for me. I wanted to be in the very midst of that light, didn't want to stop looking at it. That fact that I had a difficult time removing my eyes from said light reinforced that train of thought.

In the next instant, the siren wind increased, howling from the northwest, bringing swirls of snow that reminded me of the night I'd been a temporary hood ornament for that eighteen-wheeler. As winter wound its way around me, I realized I didn't feel cold at all. I also realized I was inexplicably now standing on the first step of the enormous wraparound porch enveloping the house.

Standing. On two legs.

In a split second, I reached down to my left leg and felt for flesh that had been AWOL for over twelve days. It sort of reminded me of my first date with Kara and trying to get to second base. My fingers had hurt for a week.

To my surprise, what I felt wasn't flesh at all, but some sort of metal that felt strong but of light weight. I pulled my hand back, waited a few moments and then gave into my curiosity. I attempted to pull up the leg of the trousers but couldn't. The pants were held fast inside the high boots I wore.

I was considering my options on how to remove my pant leg so I could get to the bottom of this mystery, snow or not, when the door began to open.

I snapped erect with unsettling apprehension, recalling the wet hobo outfit those long years ago and holding fast to the hope against a repeat performance, as I waited for the door to reveal the house's residents.

My wait was short.

The small, slightly bent woman, whose advanced age was immediately obvious, shuffled a few steps onto the porch. I tilted my head, trying to get a good glimpse of her face, but shadows prevented me from doing so.

"Gabriel. It's been a long time," she said.

Her voice wasn't anything I expected. It was smooth, fluent, young, and extremely pleasant. And she was mistaken. I'd remember a voice like that. People who spend a lot of time on the phone know what I'm talking about.

"How long, ma'am?"

"Well, I suppose that's a matter of perception."

Great, more riddles. She must be Samuel's older sister.

"What does that mean? And please speak slowly; I'm getting my sanity handed to me in a basket here."

She smiled. I couldn't see it so much, actually, but felt it. Her aura, which I hadn't noticed until that very second, began to glow a comforting teal. A color I'd not seen to date. I suspected there was going to be a boatload of aura variations coming around the corner. Even though I didn't know why I thought that.

"My name is Mary. Come in. We must talk before you leave for the next part of this journey."

Ready to indulge in another smartass remark, I refrained. I felt a sense of respect for this old woman that made me think twice; besides, I wanted to get inside. She was one intriguing reason for that, but that almost-living light on the third floor was really pulling at me.

Taking one step up with my left leg, I then lifted the right, lost my balance for a brief moment, recovered, and finished that step. I repeated my motions to the top of the stoop, each step with less trepidation and increasing balance.

"Hey, I—"

The old woman's face was now in plain view. Her eyes were a soft green, perhaps even jade. Her long, white hair was thick, framing a still beautiful face, despite the long scar that cascaded over her left cheek, stopping at the corner of her full mouth. As interesting a sight as that was, something else grabbed my voice and held it captive.

This woman—who I now understood was the helper with a secret, the one Samuel had spoken of and subsequently sent me to—was also the face of the ancient woman I'd seen just before the truck had sent me to coma world.

After another rousing bout with my recent slack-jaw malady, I recovered.

"Who are you?" I demanded.

Those inescapable eyes fixed on mine, searching so deeply I felt almost violated, but in a pleasant, honest way.

Strange description, I know. You had to be there.

In an instant I felt as if she knew every detail of my sometimes-misdirected life. Disconcerting didn't cover what was prancing through my apparently transparent thoughts. Yet, I felt no condemnation from her. I, on the other hand, needed a good brain scrub as again I recalled a few of my most fallible moments, aside from that peacock thing.

I suspect we all perform those totally asinine, incomprehensible acts that cause us to shake our heads later in life. Those actions, however, serve a purpose, adding humility to our lives. If, at that moment, I could have been any more humble, I'd be a naked Hindu monk begging for money on the front steps of a Catholic church.

Ever so slowly, she reached up, kissing me on the cheek, and then took my hands in her own, her aura spiking almost as bright as Kara's had when she was doing that kissy-face number all over my face.

"Why, Gabe, my name is Mary and I'm your real mother."

8-CHAPTER

"If you don't close your mouth, Gabe, you'll need a snow shovel to breathe," she said.

She was right. I steadied myself and closed my mouth. But it didn't stay closed long; that would have been impossible.

"Mother? What? You're not my mother. I remember her very well, thank you, and she's not you. She loved me. She took care of me. I never saw you while growing up."

I paused, reflecting on the paradox of my words and my spirit, which were battering back and forth. She was wrong and right.

Mothers can be far different than moms, yes?

The cascade of words, my words, began again.

"I . . . I know you, however. I saw you just before my accident. Well, your face, and now you're right here. And real, but my mother? Not," I managed.

A genius with words, I am.

Her smile grew as she grasped my hand and led me into the haunted house that had been part of the wonderful mysteries of my youth.

"Let's talk, Gabe."

If she'd been walking straight into the fires of hell, I would have followed her. Her touch was like that of my deceased mother, my grandmother, and Kara wrapped all into one living phenomena. We were related, there was no doubt, but I had no inclination how, despite her alarming claim of being my mother.

Entering the room, she released my hand and moved gingerly toward two red velvet, high-back Victorian chairs bordered with ornate mahogany wood setting at opposite forty-five degree angles mere feet in front of the fireplace.

The delightful combined scent of burning cherry and maple wood were almost as enticing as the anticipated comfort of those chairs and the ensuing rational (I hoped) discussion.

After the whirlwind of the last few hours, I could use a little calming comfort. Throw in a useful clarification or ten, and we might have something going. I could market it as the three Cs—calm, comfort, clarify—using this woman's image on the CD, providing I survived whatever came next . . . and there was most certainly something coming next. Samuel had said it, this woman knew it, and I felt it.

She settled into the chair on the right, the flames casting a subtle shade of copper on her profile. It somehow made her appear older, but didn't squelch the steady glow of her aura.

Kara and I had journeyed on three Caribbean cruises in our lives, and one of the most stunning attributes of that world is the aqua-teal color of the water, brilliant and clear over the white-sand bottoms surrounding the islands. Remarkable, soothing, and enchanting all rolled into one.

Her aura was now the very essence of that hue, yet even more vivid than when I'd first noticed it. This time, I felt no urge to force it out of my line of sight. She and the aura were one, it seemed, rendering that act totally unnecessary.

Pulling the tattered shawl from the arm of the chair, she covered her lap and then folded her hands over it, her gaze boring directly though my eyes and into my soul again. Dramatic? Perhaps, but it's as close to truth as I can muster.

"Well, you are the fine man I thought you'd become, but before we discuss what you obviously doubt is real, let me answer three pressing questions that I would ask if I were in your position."

"Only three? That's all I get? That's like getting one Lay's potato chip."

That mesmerizing smile returned. "I said three *pressing* questions, Gabe."

"You did. Fire away."

"Yes. I'm your real biological mother."

My countenance must have revealed the ever-present doubt inside my head. She waved away my sour face with a curl of her hand.

"Let me explain. I owe that to you. In 1971, my husband was killed in the Vietnam War. I loved him so very much. We were the very essence of soulmates. Much like you and Kara."

Her eyes averted to the fireplace for a moment as she fought for control of her sadness and despair. I knew this because I sensed those emotions in her. I was struck with what an amazing love they must have shared to still feel like that some forty-five years later.

She turned back to me. "I buried him and then proceeded to stay in this house, leaving only for groceries every few weeks, for the next ten years. His pension and life insurance were plenty for a woman like me so there was no real need to do anything but mourn. Then, on my fiftieth birthday, I decided to go out to celebrate. I was still in pain over losing Paul, but thought it time to try to get on with what was left of my life."

Repositioning her hands, she continued.

"I dressed to the hilt and then walked into the Eastside Bar. I sat at a corner table and ordered a bottle of Scotch and began my night out. After two drinks, I was joined by a younger, tall, good-looking man who specialized, it seemed, in smooth talk and a talent for drinking without becoming sloshed."

"I know those kind," I said.

"I didn't. The next morning, I awoke at the hotel on the south end of town, alone, with a headache and the realization that I had done something totally out of my realm of thinking. I drove home, that knowledge akin to shame, and did my best to relinquish the guilt that had taken over my mind. I felt like I'd cheated on Paul and let God down."

I was becoming completely enthralled by her story, but felt the "so what" coming. Nevertheless, I wanted to help her alleviate the remorse she obviously still harbored.

"My brother Luke, delusional as he is sometimes, talks about God's grace being the great equalizer to our mistakes. If you believe that stuff."

"Your brother would be right, even if you don't believe that stuff."

She stood and shuffled to me. Reaching down, she lifted my hand to her face and then traced the scar with the back of my hand, then returned to her chair.

Our souls joined a little closer, me seeing her emotional nakedness and where she was going next in this conversation. "Joined at the hip" held a new meaning for me.

How many ways can a person engulf another in their very essence? I'll let you know when I figure it out, if I'm ever able to express such a nebulous experience. I did the math. If I were truly her son, she was now in her mid-eighties. I hoped I looked as good as she did now when I turned forty, if I lived that long.

"Four months later, I realized that I wasn't going through my change, but that I was pregnant. It was so clear what had to happen next. I got into the old Ford, ate two bars of chocolate with almonds, drank a half a bottle of chardonnay, and then proceeded to drive head long into a tree along Highway 85."

"Thus the scar?"

She nodded. "I only succeeded in banging myself up. At any rate, I realized that dying with a baby in my old womb wasn't what God, or I, truly wanted, so I put myself under a doctor's care and did the best I could to stay healthy. During that time, the doctor and I, and others, searched for a family that would take my baby. In reality, I didn't want to die at all, but knew at almost fifty-one, I couldn't raise a child. Having one was difficult enough. After a few weeks of searching, the Stark family stepped up, and you were set."

Her smile returned. "You were born five months later. I did what the staff told me not to do—I couldn't help myself—and placed you on my chest anyway. While I loved that connection, I was far too pragmatic to go against what I knew was right. It was one of those heart-be-damned moments, I suppose."

I rubbed my face with both hands. There wasn't a hint of untruth in her story. I suppose I could wrestle with all of the reasons she had let me go, but hearing it from her mouth made some sense. It's a hard thing to accept for anyone—that your biological mother didn't want to keep you—but in this case, with the truth laid bare, I handled it.

"Why didn't my parents tell me?"

She shook her head. "I don't know. I suppose things were more private back then. I know they didn't think they could have children, even though you have a brother now."

I began to speak. She stopped me.

"I don't know who your father is. I didn't know, until recently, why a fifty-year-old woman was allowed to have a child she'd never raise, and I surely don't have a clue as to why your parents ended up being able to conceive your brother."

Moistening her lips, she continued. "Gabe. I simply don't know all of the whys; I just know things work for a reason, okay? But I do know you are special and the fate of North Haven and much more rests in my child's ability to fulfill his calling."

Now I *knew* she was related to Samuel.

Oddly enough, as naturally as I'd accepted that my leg was gone, I accepted her revelation about being my mother in the same vein. It just was. However, I was still working on the "you are special" idea.

She pointed to the fireplace. "Please put some more wood on the fire, and I'll answer your next question."

I obliged and sat back down. But not before I gave the small, intense glow coming from the spiral staircase over her shoulder another longing gander. I could almost hear that persistent light calling my name.

She tilted her head in my direction, smiled, and then motioned toward my left leg. "Pull the leg up on your trousers. You need to see," she said softly.

In the midst of this woman's presence, I'd virtually forgotten about the leg.

I looked down to the black pants possessing pockets, and, I might add, that fit a tad tighter than I was accustomed. You know, my legs looked pretty damned good, in the sexy way. I don't think Tina Turner has much to worry about, though.

Reaching to the top of the boot, I began to roll up the pant leg, saw the first glimmer of light on metal, stopped, exhaled, and continued.

Knowing I had lost a leg and that it was replaced with something altogether foreign to me was one thing. Actually seeing it was quite another.

Move over, Terminator. The sleek attachment replacing my lower leg was affixed above my muscular leg (Did I say I was looking pretty hot?) with a small metal band on the outside that felt lightweight, but I knew instinctively it was as tough as a Sherman tank. There were two, lower-leg metal bars wrapped around one another like some sort of DNA design. They each grew wider as they disappeared into the black boot. I had to see what my "foot" consisted of.

After removing the boot, I got my answer.

My slack-jaw propensity was becoming a bit annoying. I closed my mouth a few seconds into my inspection after I'd touched the metal replica of a skinned foot. The metal was the only true difference from the bone structure I'd seen in college biology, at least as far as I could determine.

Each joint, each intricate joining beginning with the ankle and where the tibia and fibula connected right down to the small, intricate design of the little toe phalanges was exquisite.

I wiggled my toes, and they responded as if they were the originals. A few moments later, when I was done marveling at the concept that was my new left leg, I sought her face.

"How?"

"The band around the top of your knee sends pulses, generated from the band itself as it taps into your nervous system, down through the metal bones."

"We, humans I mean, don't have technology like that, you know . . . like that," I pointed at my leg. "Do we?" I asked in another storm of brilliant articulation.

"No Gabe, humans don't, but you'd be surprised at how close humans are getting to magic like this," she said, a faint grin still lighting her face. "There's something else. Feel on the inside of your knee, there's a small indentation. Push it."

Oh, I'd heard that one before. It was right up there with "pull my finger" and "the check is in the mail."

"What happens?"

She leaned toward me. "Push it, sweetheart."

Respect your elders, they said. Do what you're told, they said. There were lots of scared kids who had been obedient to suggestions like hers.

I sighed, felt for the tiny spot that felt smooth to my touch. Keeping a steady eye on my leg, I pushed the button.

What happened next was like a sword sliding into the scabbard, except the effect was the other way around.

A flesh-colored covering, soft and strong at the same time, enveloped the metal leg in a blink, covering every contour, making the leg appear totally real.

I blinked, then reached down to touch it, tears forming quickly. Manly be damned. I knew the leg wasn't real, but it played the part incredibly well.

I glanced up to ask the next question of the hour, just in time to see the long poker from the fireplace swinging full-bore in my direction.

9-CHAPTER

I had no time to do anything but flinch, awaiting life-damaging contact from her impression of the Great Bambino's powerful homerun swing.

I couldn't help but notice her great stance, however. Hands high, legs balanced, weight on her back foot, eyes locked on the target. Impressive.

The poker hit my lower leg with a resounding wham, and I felt nothing. At least nothing that amounted to pain. There was a slight vibration and then a swish as the bottom section of the poker flew past my ear.

I scrambled to my feet, looking at her with the same surprise you'd give one of your friends who had just thumped you in the gonads for no reason other than to see you crawl on the ground.

"What the hell was that?"

Dropping the handle of the would-be weapon on the floor, she sat back down, re-covering herself with the tattered shawl.

"I wanted to make sure you trusted that leg and how it can protect you when, or if, the time is right."

I exhaled. "Mission accomplished, but you could have just said that."

"No, I couldn't have. You had to see it."

She was right again. I was sensing another pattern.

"I don't suppose you can tell me how I came to acquire this limb?"

Shaking her head, she smiled again. She seemed tired, and I could swear she was older than when I first met this mother of mine.

"I only get so much information. Just know it wasn't without great thought and by someone far more important than an old woman and one-time mother like me."

I stood, gazing at her, wondering what she thought of motherhood and parenthood in general. Important didn't cover my thoughts regarding being a parent, especially given mine and Kara's lack of children.

Did I detect some regret on her part for not trying to raise me? I suppose we all practice the nonproductive act of self-evaluation regarding only our faults and regrets and never our accomplishments, our finest moments, if you will.

Once again, as we embraced the silence, my eyes averted to the lighted flight of steps. The reflection of that luminosity glancing from the wooden banister strutted in a confident, hypnotizing rhythm that was as enticing as free pizza and beer.

Mother Mary painstakingly arose from her chair, shuffled the few steps to where I stood. Yes, I was keeping an eye on her hands. I didn't want to suffer a repeat of the leg test on my noggin. Kara had told me several times it was sufficiently hard, so I reasoned no such test was necessary.

Her aura remained the same enchanting color, but it was now considerably dimmer. I didn't care for how that felt.

Taking my hands in hers, she spoke so quietly I had to bend toward her to hear.

"The last question has to do with where you are, truly. I can come close to explaining that, but I think you'd be better served by taking the stairs that call your name, Gabriel."

"Then what?"

Yet, I was already imagining myself taking those steps two at a time.

"You'll figure it out. Let me say this. You are in North Haven, but you're not."

"That helps," I smiled, knowing what she was trying to say, sort of.

"I suppose it doesn't at that. This state, this place you are in is much like dreaming while you're wide awake. I suppose folks would call it parallel worlds or even different dimensions. It's neither, but both. This realm is just out of reach for most humans to see, yet it affects us profoundly each day."

I know, I know. But in a weird paradoxical way, she made sense. I remembered the comment Samuel had made concerning the fight between good and evil, and immediately knew this path was on the way to the main stage for a powerful war.

Wow. Listen to me. Was I starting to believe her and Samuel?

"I sense that you have some understanding already. Good. But understanding won't be enough, Gabriel. You've had your spirit, as well as your eyes, opened a fraction, but to survive and to fulfill your purpose, you'll have to embrace what's next for you."

"What does—?"

She hushed me with a finger to the lips, kissed me on the cheek, and pointed to the staircase.

"I don't have any more answers. It's time," she said. "I gave you what I have. I pray the knowledge will be purposeful and serve you when you need it. I love you, Gabriel."

I couldn't speak. I choke up at weddings and Detroit Lions wins sometimes, so this emotional setting wasn't easy, especially in light of how this whole seer situation caused me to sense things more deeply. I sensed her love as pure.

I kissed her on the head and hurried past her to what she and Samuel termed as "next."

I put my foot on the first step and turned back for one last look at a mother I'd never known. And, make no mistake, "last look" was correct because I knew I'd never see this woman again.

Too late. She was no longer there.

All that I could see was a dying fire and two dust-covered chairs that looked as if no one had touched them in decades. I should have been surprised and even freaked out by the scene that now had taken on a far different view than I had left moments ago. Yet, there was no surprise. Only acceptance.

I hate it when I'm this calm. That usually comes after the fourth or fifth hard cider.

Lingering for a few seconds longer, I wanted to go back to the hearth to find her, or at least get a clue as to where she'd gone, but I knew that would be complete folly. Mother Mary was on her way to her own "next."

Bowing low, I then stood erect and blew her a kiss anyway, hoping she could see me even though I could not see her. Mother is still mother, no matter the circumstances surrounding her estrangement from me.

I turned toward the second story of this beautiful old home and bounded up the steps with a dexterity I hadn't possessed perhaps ever.

Maybe I should get two of these new leg puppies.

I stopped at the threshold of the door leading to the lighted room calling my name, abruptly aware of the scent of lilac and sulfur rolled into one. Both of these pointed odors brought back memories of certain stages in my life.

One, the lilac reminded me of home and the Michigan springs I love greatly. Clear, clean, and full of new life set the bar high, even through the cool temperatures.

The sulfur brought back something else entirely. An incident I'd buried regarding the house fire that had almost killed all of us on that hot summer night years ago.

No, I hadn't started it, but I suspect that was the last effort my younger brother gave to smoking cigarettes.

They were such contrasting memories, touching the extreme ends of my emotional spectrum.

Why now? Why here? Mere chance?

Reaching for the ancient doorknob, I hesitated, delaying entrance to the room that I'd previously longed to enter. I immediately realized I shouldn't have paused and just gone through the doorway.

He really was going to kill me.

Dropping to my knees, I ducked as the shimmering sword narrowly missed, accomplishing my William Wallace impression, slamming into the door casing with the authority of ten men.

I rolled to my right and turned toward the source of that swing. It was still dark in those shadows beyond the light's reach, but the unintelligible growl that accompanied the dark green aura dancing around him led me directly to this . . . being—the one who wanted my head disarticulated from my body.

"Being" was right. This man-like creature was all of nine feet tall. His muscular body was covered with coarse hair, including a long, flowing beard cut neatly and hanging down to his waist.

He wore no helmet over his shoulder-length hair, or even armor, only a short-sleeved leather top with matching loincloth fringing on massive thighs.

Immediately I was struck with how Goliath must have appeared to young King David. I doubt the young man felt his scrotum tighten as much as mine, however, given that Goliath probably didn't have four arms.

Surprisingly, I wasn't shocked by his otherworldly appearance or yet another colored aura. Chalk it up to the entire set of strange encounters I'd endured in the last few hours. That or I had been given the wrong medication and was now tripping on LSD. Either way, I knew I was in deep trouble.

The huge being moved quickly, extracting the sword from the wooden door casing and then lunging in my direction again, sword flying from his upper right arm. I jumped straight up, diving to my left, and tumbled past him, feeling one of his other enormous hands barely miss clutching my hair.

The sword struck the wide post of the stairwell with the sound of a gunshot and buried five inches deep.

"What are you doing?" I asked, my voice high as I stood, again impressed with my ability to size up the obvious.

"You must die, Seer," he growled, fumbling for the sword with all four hands. Quite interesting to watch, by the way.

His deep and surprisingly articulate voice would put James Earl Jones to shame.

"Why?" I asked. I was getting better at the whole question thing.

"Because the Master has ordered it. You cannot be allowed to join your Triad. I, Trench, must kill you," he answered.

"Trench? That's your name?"

"Don't mock me, fragile one, as it is the last name you'll hear this side of hell."

"What did I do to you and your master?"

"You were born. That is enough. Just stand there for a few more moments, and I will do what I do quickly."

I wanted to continue to play twenty questions, but he was now bent over the sword and pulling with all of his might. The sword would be free momentarily to cut me six ways from Sunday.

Time to hit the road.

I reached for the door and the pulsating light I was sure would save me. God knew I wanted to live and to be saved. I twisted the knob, then I stopped, a surge of anger escalating inside of me. I was suddenly tired of having people swing trucks, swords, and pokers at me. Really tired of it.

I took three strides and kicked my attacker's backside, which was sticking out away from his loincloth (I guess his people didn't have a Hanes factory) with all of my strength, extending my left leg fully.

The effect was astounding. The colossal creature, this Trench, flew over the railing, four arms flailing, swearing in a dialect I didn't understand just as he removed the five-foot sword from its wooden prison, sending it high into the air.

He twisted in midflight, dark surprise registering on his face, his puke-green aura bright, as he tumbled toward the bottom of the spiraling stairs. The large sword followed him on his journey downward.

In an instant, it was over. The crash was tremendous, yet the following silence more acute.

I peered over the disintegrated railing, breathing hard, and took in the unexpected sight of my attacker's fate as he lay on his back.

The long blade was now protruding through his massive chest, dark blood forming a crimson pool underneath his leather-clad body and slowly seeping into his beard. His black eyes were open but not seeing, his aura a thing of the past.

One never knew anything for sure in this eccentric world I was tramping through, but he sure as taxes looked dead.

Whoa. I'd just killed someone, or something, even though it wasn't without cause. And I got lucky to see a few more seconds of my own life. Who could plan what had happened to good old Trench?

Still, I wanted to feel something horrible. Guilt, fear, shock, even relief, for having taken the life of another, no matter the circumstances.

None of those sensations expressed themselves to me. Instead, I was smacked with a perception of . . . dare I say, victory? I was still breathing and massive Trench was not.

How low on the Vegas oddsmaker's sheet is that?

Staring at the being below me drove home the idea that death, just like life, was universal, no matter what realm we walked. Trench was now in his version of the afterlife, wherever that may exist, if at all. I had to admit, though, the ideas of other planes of existence was at least becoming more tangible.

Good God. I was thinking about realms and other such crap and felt totally at peace with all of it. The journey to the bizarre was complete. Well, it would be when I woke up in the hospital bed.

Man, did I have a story to tell. Maybe I'll become a writer.

My new career possibilities went on hold as it came to mind what Trench had said.

What the hell did he mean the Triad? Who was the Master? Why did he want my head in a basket? Did I really want to know? I suspected wanting, in this case, and getting were going to be two entirely different mindsets.

Time would tell.

After mooning Old Trench and then giving him the finger as an added measure of complete victory, I moved away from the edge of the stairs and grasped the engraved handle of the door I'd first come up the stairs to investigate.

As I stood there, my hand on the knob, I was struck with another one of those epiphany moments.

I began to accept that this upcoming trek was beyond what even Samuel and Mary had been able to describe or, at the very least, what I could get my mind around. I think seeing Trench in all of his glory had at least pounded one more nail into the coffin of belief, no matter what my smartass side was espousing.

This war, the battle, or whatever, was for real and for keeps. I, Gabriel Andrew Starks, was finally ready to find out what that meant exactly.

So be it.

I turned the handle and stepped into the light.

10-CHAPTER

When I was a child, my dad used to watch reruns of a seventies comedy called *Hee Haw*. It was incredibly corny, showcasing old bad jokes, banjos, country music, Junior Sample, and some hot women in frayed jean short-shorts lying around in make-believe haystacks. I think those women were the real reason my dad tuned into that show.

At any rate, some of the regular male stars would do this skit each week featuring a song with dubious lyrics that said: "If it weren't for bad luck, I'd have no luck at all. Gloom, despair, and agony on me."

The chorus from that less than artistic composition epitomized my next step in this trip.

After my eyes adjusted to the flood of brightness that was in contrast to the shadows of the hallway in the old house, I took in my new, barren environment.

I wasn't in an antiquated room at all, but rather, the door had led me into the presence of a vast sea of white sand that ran directly into a deep blue horizon. I'd seen pictures of deserts like this. They weren't on my bucket list. Ever.

I triple swore and did it quite well, if I say so myself. Surprise, surprise. What did I expect at this stage? Normal? A room with a gourmet buffet and kegs the size of water towers?

My first instinct was to turn back, exit this wasteland wannabe, and call the whole thing off. Seer be damned. They, whoever they were, could have this broken, messed up rock we call Earth. I wanted a steak and something stiff to drink.

With that in mind, I pivoted toward the door, reaching for where the handle should have been.

I could only stare.

The desert, in all of its pale glory, stretched behind me as well, as endless as it was before me. There was most certainly no doorway, door knob, or even a well-crafted brass door knocker in the shape of Jacob Marley's profile—although that image wouldn't have surprised me in the least.

I stepped back as if that would allow me a better look at what wasn't there to begin with.

Nope. Nothing. Nada. After fighting off the next step in my panic evolution, realizing that would only make things worse—as if that were even possible—I tried something more practical.

I closed my eyes and pretended I was blind so that the door would feel sorry for me and reappear.

Nope.

Letting loose a pent-up breath, I prayed for a six-pack of Angry Orchard cider.

After waiting a few moments, I looked around and, not seeing a waitress coming my way, I began to survey more closely the other-worldly landscape that held me in its palm and apparently in its near future, at the minimum.

My hair ruffled at the slightest of breezes that also caused some delicate wisps of sand to tango across the landscape. The patterns in the fine sand were almost fun to watch. That breeze also carried with it an unusual aroma, immediately reminding me of the combined scents of lilac and sulfur, as I'd experienced in the hallway of the Victorian.

Once was a chance encounter. Twice was not a coincidence. Maybe in this desert, the wind carried the essence of a peculiar flower or plant. Although possible, I didn't truly think that was the case. I suspected something far more intricate and perhaps sinister at work, but decided not to dwell on it.

I read once that the day, this very moment, holds enough trouble without inviting more. All in all, that is good wisdom.

I shaded my eyes from the brightness of the clear, bluish sky, although the hue was a tad deeper than I remembered seeing back home, with its pleasant richness, and turned away from the high sun. I wanted to focus on anything near or in the distance that would give me some perspective. I could see that I was standing on a dune flanked by two others, forming a triangle, and that gave me a high point from which to scan the area.

There were a few plants or trees, at least green protrusions in the sand, but nothing that resembled a building, a highway, or even a billboard telling me it was only fifty miles to Vegas. That would have worked because I know for a fact they have liquor in that little town.

Dropping my hand, I frowned. There was something else going on here. It wasn't hellish hot as the environment dictated it should be.

I'd taken that trip to Vegas and had booked one of those tours out to the desert with Kara. My sweat had sweated, then it evaporated almost as quickly as it had formed on my arms and face.

Not the case here. All signs indicated tremendous heat should be the order of the day, especially the fact that the sun was almost directly overhead, yet it was comfortable without the sensation of the sun beating on your brow. Another anomaly for me to ponder.

I thought my head would burst if I experienced one more of these counterintuitive situations.

One last time, I scanned where the door should have been and observed nothing but white sand and a few small, obscure plants.

Did I say I could use a drink?

"You can't stay here forever," I finally said out loud, while I did a complete one-eighty, trying to decide which direction would allow me to live longer.

Then I saw it out of the corner of my eye. There was slight movement to my left, smack on top of one of the other dunes.

There was a small crack in the very fabric of the air, disrupting the landscape. It was as if someone, or something, had used a meat cleaver to rip a slit in the very air itself. I crossed my arms. This was going to be good. Or not.

The gash disappeared only to reappear in a micro-moment. The opening grew wider and seemed to extend about seven feet into the air. The sharp edge of the opening told me it was not some random articulation of a tear, but an intelligently designed phenomenon. It slammed shut again, reopened even wider as the sound of voices, unintelligible to me, rose to a climaxing crescendo.

Then, as if by magic, she stood on the crest of the pale dune, orange aura in full splendor. There was no entranceway, door, or double-secret hatch to show how she'd gotten to that spot on top of the dune. Not unlike my own experience.

That, however, was now taking a back seat to the appearance of the female some sixty feet to my left.

My mouth stayed closed this time. I was adapting to this Gene Roddenberry world.

The skin covering this tall female held a bluish tint, accented by a shock of long, darker blue hair running past her waist. Her features were not cute in that Sally Field way, but possessed a rare beauty that I was sure had broken more than one heart, if they indeed had hearts where she hailed from.

This curvy, certainly not dainty, humanoid had large hands with six-fingers affixed to each, large gold rings on the middle three fingers of both hands. She carried some sort of instrument that held me clueless, as usual on this journey, in her left hand. She possessed what looked like an alien version of a crossbow in her right. I was thankful that she had the proper number of limbs.

Oddly enough, she was wearing black attire very similar to mine, except I didn't have the shiver of metal arrows, and her boots were way cooler, rising up to her knees and embroidered with oval ringlets.

Our eyes met, mine blue, hers startling fuchsia, and I'd swear we shared the same thoughts.

Well, almost. I didn't think I could kick *her* ass in a fair fight, but we liked each other's hair.

I began to ask her name and stopped. I already knew it.

"Sabrea," I said. "You're Sabrea."

Her face contorted in surprise and accompanying confusion. She then spoke a few words that I was at an utter loss to understand, except for one.

Gabriel.

We began an uneasy, yet natural walk toward each other, not taking our eyes from one another, but more from curiosity than fear. Still, I felt some trepidation from her. Her aura and what it showed me confirmed my suspicions.

I didn't know what this Amazon specimen would have to fear from me. Yet the unknown, and I was that to her, breeds caution at the minimum.

Sabrea was taller than me by six inches, her teeth white, her canines longer than humans, but not quite animal length, her arms bigger than my guns.

I think I have more hair on my chest, though.

We stopped within a couple of feet of one another. She studied my face, her aura steady, then she slowly reached down and traced my chin and cheekbones with the second index finger of her right hand. Her touch was tender, yet I felt the strength that was hers.

After touching my ears, eyes, and schnozzle, and then running her hand through my hair, I saw the beginnings of a smile form on her full lips. If I believed she was beautiful before that innocent gesture, I was wrong. There had to be a word that rose above beauty, but I couldn't grab hold of it.

"Thank you, Gabriel. You are pleasant to behold as well, in a human sort of way."

Her voice was strong, but certainly feminine. I would call it a trifle sexy even.

Hey, she thought I was pleasant to look at. Wait until I tell the guys at the pub.

Hold on. Her voice? I could understand her.

"How did you do that? How can I understand you now?"

"I did nothing, Gabriel. It is you and your gift, Seer."

Okay. I would have known if I'd done something to facilitate converting a completely alien language to perfect English.

"What? I—"

Seer. The gift that keeps on giving.

Samuel and Mother Mary both had hinted that the ability to see and read auras, and possibly the heart's intent of others, was only a start to what the gift might bring. They'd both said I was special. That endorsement was just short of *"The Force is strong with this one,"* but it would do for me.

In any event, I knew she was right. The need for us to communicate was essential—for some reason still unknown to me—but by reading each other's thoughts, we'd built a link between us that included breaking the language barrier.

No, I don't get it . . . yet. I'm only aware that I'm right and it works.

"I sense that you're right."

"I am. You shall discover that I am always correct."

Great. I'm not even married to this one.

"Truly?"

"Yes."

Then her head flew back as she laughed loudly in a captivating dirge that would have made Nixon smile.

"I am joking, Gabriel. But you will need to trust me, as will I you, when the moments present themselves."

An alien with a sense of humor. God be praised. This was far better than something wanting to eat my brain.

"Funny girl," I said, returning the laugh.

She bowed her head, still smiling, almost like a shy schoolgirl who'd just told her first successful joke.

"I like you, Seer. You are a good soul. A little puny, but you cannot help that."

"Is that right?" I asked without a trace of ill will.

"Oh, it is. I told you, I'm always right." Another brilliant smile accompanied her statement.

Can folks bond in less than three minutes? It must be so because I already had deep affection for her. Her heart was pure, her very essence a symbol of integrity. More than that, she was passionate about what she was, even though I didn't know what that involved exactly.

Reaching up, I touched her face, cementing our bond even further.

"Sabrea, I need to know what all of this means. I have bits and pieces, but the big picture eludes me."

Her hair flowed in perfect rhythm as she nodded slowly.

"Is there not evil where you come from?"

Where I come from? Was her question metaphoric for who in the name of Heaven would live in Northern Michigan other than those of us native to the area? Or was she talking about another planet or something?

Opening my mouth to dig deeper into her statement, I hesitated. It would be my turn to ask questions shortly. I somehow knew that.

"Of course. Samuel asked me sort of the same question."

"Ahh, Samuel. He seems to get around."

"You've met?"

"We have—"

"As have we."

Turning away from Sabrea in sheer panic because I recognized that deep bass voice, I laid eyes on the being who'd spoken.

Apparently a five-foot sword in the chest hadn't done the trick.

Trench, four arms churning, was steaming over the sand in our direction.

11-CHAPTER

Confusion had been a major player in my life since the accident (some would argue that was the case prior), and this situation was the crème de la crème.

"Run, Sabrea," I yelled in a high-pitched, scaredy-cat voice, then I fell flat as I tried to gain footing on the sand.

"Why would we run, Gabriel?" she asked as I lifted to my feet.

"Why? He's going to kill us."

"Gabriel. . . ."

Too late. I felt his breath on my neck as his shadow engulfed my own. Outsized and out-armed, I was going down, but I wasn't succumbing like a lamb to slaughter.

I whirled, leg in the air, to face the giant who'd sworn to kill me for a plethora of reasons. It's funny how facing death, again, brought out more fight than flight in me. I'd always pictured myself as a lover. Well, sort of. I just didn't care for fighting all that much.

Once we were face to face, still a bit in awe at his size, I drew my leg back to make a eunuch of him, hoping his gonads were located in the usual vicinity between the two swords dangling at his hips and just above the leather pouch around his midsection. If not, well, you figure it out.

But Trench moved far swifter than I. One of his massive arms snaked out and held the leg firm as he pulled me so close I could count the crow's feet at the corners of his eyes and smell his breath, which wasn't so bad actually. I'd figured him for a raw meat kind of guy.

Wait. Something was amiss.

His aura matched Sabrea's in orange color and intensity. I hadn't recalled an aura like this in my first encounter with him, for one thing. For another, his great dark eyes were filled with curiosity, not malignant violence. And he was smaller, not by much, but he was.

"You're not Trench," I stated.

"No, I am not, Gabriel. He was from my tribe, but we have, or had, far different visons of what is just and worth fighting for."

"I'm personally grateful for that." I hopped up and down on my right leg to keep my balance.

He released my limb, steadied me, and then began to examine me with a gentleness that seemed impossible for one with his intimidating appearance.

He finally shook his head, wonder in his eyes. "How did one as you vanquish such a great warrior?"

I stood taller. I wasn't *that* much of wimp.

"I was a little lucky. He went over a railing after I'd kicked him—and I did kick him hard because I'm that kind of mean—and his sword buried in his chest. How do you know about all that? It just happened."

"Mean? If you say it is so, Seer. I suspect it was less luck than you realize. And time and space are not the same for each of us. His death is well announced. Our tribe rejoiced at the news. I fear his master did not, however."

There it was again. "What master?"

He frowned at me as if I'd asked a question that a preschooler should be able to answer, and then ignored my inquiry.

"First, you must learn of us, my tribe. Use your gift, Seer."

Good idea. I might get more answers that way.

I reached out and touched his lower left arm, concentrated, and let this powerful being speak to me in a fashion I was growing accustomed to.

His name was Arzur. His tribe, the Bansha, was part of an order that made societal sense, but made my heart ache simultaneously.

He, and those born like him physically, were immediately placed in an environment designed for warrior development. Four arms meant warrior, plain and simple, and there was no negotiation from that fate.

Intellect, artistic ability, creativity, and even their capacity to distinguish right from wrong were ignored because that was for others born with different characteristics, which didn't include four arms and nine feet of meaty flesh. There was more, and it tied directly to his anguish as a warrior and how his heart of hearts longed for a different fate—

Suddenly the "more" was hidden from me.

"Arzur?" I asked, searching his face.

"My heart, Seer, is mine. I underestimated how you have progressed with your gift. I do not want you to see that deeply into my true nature."

It was almost comical to see this giant avert his eyes from mine, then recover his composure and remember what he was trained to be.

"So you can cut off how much I can see?"

"For now, but you are exceptional and will grow stronger," he answered. "Soon no one will be able to hide their purposes from you."

The way he articulated that idea caused my heart to leap, and not in such a great way either. Some things should stay hidden in the crevices of any being's existence, in my estimation, and there is certainly such a thing as TMI. For example, I didn't want to know about Arzur's sex life. Ever.

Stepping forward, Sabrea stretched out both hands, palms up, and smiled at Arzur. "I have sensed the same regarding our seer, Warrior," she offered.

What came next was extraordinary, at least to me.

Arzur the Warrior pivoted in her direction, as if he'd abruptly realized that we weren't alone. He bowed with all the grace that his six-hundred-pound body could muster.

His front leg straight out, his arms, all of them, tucked close to his waist, his head tilted in her direction . . . and his face broke into one of those grins that told you he hadn't smiled much during his long life. The attempt, however, was valiant.

I felt like I was at the eighteenth-century gathering of a Scottish clan, where the warriors swore their allegiance to the laird of the lands. Awkward, yet I've not seen many acts in my life more sincere.

"Fair navigator, it is good to finally meet you. Arzur at you service."

Their auras grew brighter as they clasped hands around wrists and nodded in acknowledgment of each other.

Glancing at Sabrea, then back to Arzur, I watched their interaction with curiosity while they naturally accepted each other and this impossible rendezvous with an expectant attitude that I didn't possess. It was as if they'd met before, but I knew they hadn't. Not like this.

For a moment, I felt a twinge of envy at their greeting. Maybe I could show them a high-five and that defining act would make me cool too.

I resisted. Maybe raising my hand high to these two meant that I wanted to be a eunuch or Arzur's girlfriend. I kept my hand down and moved to the next logical step in this odd meeting.

All of my questions, especially the ones only shadowing the truth, needed to be answered. Now.

"It is time to talk," I said.

Arzur and Sabrea immediately stepped in my direction, settling just inches on each side of me. And I thought my big Lab, Apollo, had no sense of personal space.

"Let us talk then, Seer," said Arzur.

"But not at this location," said Sabrea, searching the sky.

"Why not here?" I asked.

"So many questions for someone with such knowledge, Gabriel."

My frustration reached its peak. Riddles from Samuel, new legs, doors that were gateways to wherever the hell this was, four arms on a Goliath lookalike, blue skin on a very hot chick, white sand, and no cold adult beverages had taken their individual tolls.

"I DON'T have knowledge. If I did, I wouldn't feel like a cat in a dog pound. I'm tired of having my questions answered with questions. I don't know squat about anything. Got it? So we're not leaving here until I have answers. Starting with where is here?"

My two new friends looked at each other, then to me. Arzur stroked his beard with all four hands, trying to get a fix on my emotions, that much I felt.

Sabrea, tilting her head, wore a wry look that was somewhere between humor and, dare I say, admiration. I got that much from her.

"Very well, Gabriel. We have time for a brief conversation. It is not good for us to be in this area for long," said Sabrea.

"About time. Where are we?"

"We are in my reality. My realm."

"That doesn't help. Go on."

She sighed and took my hand in hers. Six fingers was even weirder wrapped around my much smaller mitt.

"The universe is made up of many mysteries, Gabriel. While some on your plane know of other realities, most think such places are fairytales. But, obviously, that is not true. Along this plane of existence are many realms—dimensions, if you will—and you are now in the one that I call home."

What the hell? Might as well play along until the psych ward folks get here.

"How many of these realms are there?"

"I do not know. I only know that beings from three other realities exist."

"So when I walked through that gateway in the old house, I stepped into this world, so to speak?"

"That is correct, almost. This reality is different, but the same Earth."

My mouth fell open again, despite Mother Mary's warning. This time it could be sand instead of snow filling my pie hole.

I was standing on Earth with these two inhuman beings I could have only dreamed of encountering, yet it wasn't any place I'd seen on *my* Earth. Maybe Caribbean Rum would be more in order than hard cider.

"This is Earth?" I asked, my voice shaky even to me.

"*My* Earth," she answered softly.

"Parallel worlds then?"

She shook her head, her hair doing that slow-flowing dance again.

"No. We are all much closer than that. In a parallel world, embodying decisions made affect only that world. Not so here."

I contemplated that truth, and it was truth, no question.

Dimensions that were so closely related that decisions made on one plane affected the others? But that would be insane. There would be hundreds of political choices alone made each day that would blow this thought to kingdom come.

"Are you telling me that a leader's decision on the color of his palace or what he or she eats for dinner causes issues for other realities? That makes no sense."

She waved her blue hand. "Not those kind of decisions, Gabriel. Think. Separate the physical from the ideal."

The reach of her words finally thumped home to me. I got what she was saying, at least a little.

"What are you talking about? Good versus evil? Kindness and cruelty? Compassion and malevolence? The conditions of the heart that Samuel was talking about, is that right?"

"Yes! We are not bound by the landscape we abide in, but by the principals that truly rule the universe," she said, her fuchsia eyes sparkling.

By now, my head had stopped spinning as I concentrated on her brightening aura. That simple act caused what she'd said to ring in more truth, if she hadn't already convinced me.

I nodded slowly.

"Okay. I got it. So does that mean the loony bin folks aren't looking for me?"

"If you mean that you are not crazy after all, that could be true. But that has yet to be determined, Gabriel. You know all of what we have discussed. You simply have to believe you are what you are called to be. Trust the gift and do not block it with feeble understanding of what you observe in the natural. Should I distract you by removing my clothing so that you can think in another direction other than the one that says you are out of your normal mind?"

That would be interesting. I, however, am a gentleman, mostly.

"No, no, no. I'm listening."

"That is good, Seer. At least you are a male who will listen and ask questions instead of being distracted by unimportant issues. Do you ask for directions as well?"

Her grin made me give up one of my own. Aside from that, her encouragement rang true.

"Okay, I'll try to get my mind in order. Meanwhile, what does all of that have to do with us, and how we got here?"

Before she could answer, the sand below us exploded, and I was hurtling through the earthly, yet alien space.

12-CHAPTER

A strong hand plucked me from the air and held me, but Arzur and I continued our version of wingless flight.

Sabrea was soaring just to our right. Twisting in midflight, she'd somehow managed to pull the exotic crossbow from her shoulder and load six arrows on the clip rising above the trigger—all before we hit the sand on the backside of the three dunes where we'd been standing.

I saw the touchdown coming and tucked my head, trying to roll on the fine white grains.

I wish my home golf course had this kind of sand in the traps. I'd be a better bunker player.

Doing a fairly good job of scuttling to my feet after a decent landing, unhurt for a change, I saw that my companions were already up, both posed in classic warrior stances facing the crest some twenty feet above us.

"What was that?"

Again, with the questions.

"That, Gabriel, was why we should have left the dune and sought shelter," said Sabrea.

"I know, you're always right."

Her laugh was every bit as enchanting as her wondrous smile.

"You do learn quickly, Seer."

I had that going for me.

"To answer your question, our enemy, the one who embraces the evil who would destroy us, doesn't want us to complete the formation of this Triad. We were attacked by Culroids, foot soldiers for the evil one," said Arzur.

"But I didn't see anything. I—"

"Perhaps you should do what you are called to do, now," interrupted Arzur.

He was right.

Stepping between them, I concentrated on who or what was coming. The instantaneous rush of hatred and fear hammered me so firmly that I staggered back as the horde of dark thoughts infiltrated my own. Maybe "thoughts" wasn't quite right, more like an invasion of my very essence.

Does anyone else get this? Sometimes throughout my life, I have sensed a smothering, disconcerting evil emanating from someone, or even someplace, one so creepy that I instantly want to remove myself from that abominable situation and pray for no nightmares.

Times that by a billion, and that's what I felt in my bones regarding these Culroids. The rush of abhorrence created a new level of fear in me that I'd not witnessed in my lifetime. Something told me it wouldn't be the last of it either.

Regaining my posture, and some of my courage, I blocked just enough of the loathing and sought an aura.

One must be careful what one seeks.

The concentrated cloud of deep, menacing purple rising to our left would have been fascinating if hadn't been so ominous. It grew as the sounds of approaching warriors intensified.

Too bad, I sort of like purple . . . but not this shade and not this manifestation.

"They're coming over that part of our ridge in about thirty seconds. There are maybe fifteen of them, and they have a very large weapon, sort of like a cannon, but it concentrates light. So I guess that makes it a laser from where I come from," I said.

"Laser is unfamiliar to me, but concentrated light is not. We call it a burst saber. I suspect the effect is identical," said Arzur, shifting toward the coming onslaught. "Your warning will allow us to take them off guard for a moment. It is all we will need."

Good for them, but I wanted to help. I dug into my pockets.

Nope. No sword, no crossbow, no pistol, or switchblade. Not even a paperclip. I went from feeling part of them to helpless in a nanosecond.

I stepped closer to them.

"What do I do? I've got no weapon, and I doubt these attackers are going to bend over and let me kick them in the ass."

"You are not a warrior, Gabriel. That is not your role. We will handle this," said Sabrea without looking my way.

We were running out of time. They were about to crest that hill, and I'd be forced to hide my head in the sand as the fight was brought to us. Hell, I didn't even know why we were going to battle, did I?

But then again, I did. Destroying evil for the sake of good never gets old. I wasn't going to be left out of this one, even though I wasn't the bravest of warriors.

Hell no.

Fronting her, I touched her crossbow. Our eyes met.

"You are a navigator. You'll lead us in the direction we will need to go. But you also fight for your cause, yes? You must offer me the same opportunity."

If Freya, queen of the mythical Valkyries, had been blue, she would have no doubt carried herself the way Sabrea did at that moment. A warrior woman who loved life, relished the battle, and laughed at everything because she feared nothing.

"You are a unique seer, Gabriel Stark," she said, grinning so wide that those great white canines would give Old Drac a run for his money.

She bent and kissed me on the forehead.

"Special, undeniably."

Is it acceptable for seers to blush? I hope so. "We'll talk about seers as a whole later if we live. I want to help with the living part."

Arzur and Sabrea exchanged looks.

Ha. I got part of what was going on. I waited.

"I say give it to him, Arzur," she said, focusing back on the ridge.

The first trickle of sand rolled down our side of the embankment. Our other-worldly adversaries were seconds from showing themselves.

Arzur sighed.

"Was that a sigh, big boy? Don't sigh at me. I kicked Trench's ass. I agree with Sabrea. Give it to me."

Of course, I had no idea what I was asking, but then, in a New York second later, I did.

"You do not know how to use it, Seer. And know this, I am not Trench."

"Right. You're not. But I'm better off with it than without. And by seeing what you see, I've learned something of handling it."

"That's not enough."

"It'll have to be. Hand it over, Arzur. I've got this."

"Seers who want to fight. What will be next?"

"I don't care what's next. Give it up."

Another sigh. I was beginning to hate those sighs.

"Very well," he growled.

Without another glance in my direction, his furry lower right hand reached into his front pouch and drew out a short, gleaming sword with gold and emeralds inlaid around the ornate hilt. Rubies and what appeared to be sapphires flowed six inches down the blade and stopped in what appeared to be a symbol resembling a crucifix with a curved tail.

Eat your heart out, Samuel. This sword is far sweeter than yours.

I was almost startled by how beautiful and detailed the handiwork appeared. I instantly knew it was mine, that it was crafted for me. But God knows, even with the gleaning of some information from Arzur's mind, I had little idea what I was going to do with it.

Then again, I was sure it would come to me.

This blade wasn't a bent maple stick fitted to my small hand and used at playtime as a child when my friend, Dave Wymer, and I had vanquished many a foe, supernatural and otherwise, with a mere swipe of our versions of Excalibur. The real thing was far heavier, yet balanced and . . . just groovier.

He then flipped it in my direction. The iridescent blade rotated to the left, the sun causing it to glisten hypnotically, and I snatched it from midair (pretty sweet move) just as the first of the creatures who wanted us dead rose above the crest of the dune.

13-CHAPTER

It always amazes me when beauty is mingled with the repulsive. This sandy environment in Sabrea's world wasn't unkind to the eye. The white of it was quite settling for the most part.

The stench arising from the fifteen beings, along with their grotesque, filthy features, was the exact antithesis of that observed beauty.

There were times—after playing five or six games in a one-day softball tournament, for example—that I needed to *not* pass GO, *not* collect two hundred dollars, but instead go directly to the shower. I, in fact, during those instances, hated to drive Old Red home because I was the ultimate definition of a sweat hog and would have to shampoo her to get the stink out.

Dogs and squirrels would run from me. *I* ran from me.

But this unsavory aroma arising from the top of the dune topped any of my stink by miles. It was reminiscent of a large pig farm; however, it put even that pork institution to shame.

Throw in the uncanny resemblance of the Culroids to Sloth from that awesome movie, *The Goonies*, and I should have been shaking in my boots.

Crazy as it is, I was not.

My acceptance for this domain, hallucination or not, was gaining. I'd question events later, if there was a later for us.

I stepped next to Sabrea with Arzur to our left and crossed the sword over my chest with my right hand, bowing slightly toward the row of beings.

I then took a closer look.

These humanoid creatures were dressed in dark, tattered leather shirts and trousers that obviously were meant to be part of some uniform ensemble that had long lost any liveried significance. The stains splattered on each of their garments fed fuel to the fire that this group had killed, and often. Of course, perhaps the burgundy stains on their saber-like weapons hanging from most of their waists also helped with that deduction.

I found it interesting that none of them wore footwear on what appeared to be normal feet.

I reflected on how, toward the end of the Civil War, many Confederate soldiers wore whatever they could find because there was no more money for anything else, even going to such extremes as removing boots and clothing from their dead comrades. I suspected this group would go far beyond that protocol and actually kill a comrade for something far less.

They stared at us, their uneven eyes containing an almost lifeless quality. Despite my previously mentioned bravado, I found that a tad discomfiting.

Passion is easily dealt with, positive or negative. Dark, hopeless despair born from the type of vile existence these guys were living is far more difficult to read.

None of them moved at first, checking us out with at least the one big eye, then the middle being stepped forward, his aura darkening to almost a midnight purple. His was linked with the others, no question, but was most certainly the strongest and the most intelligent. Captain Culroid? Not to mention, he still had some hair and his eyes were only off about an inch. I bet he got far more dates than the others.

"If you drop your weapons and bow to the Master, I will make your deaths quick and precise," he said, his voice surprisingly smooth and, dare I say, human.

Why does *every* essence of evil, bad-ass killer say that?

I've seen about a million movies in my lifetime. I love all kinds, really, but action plots were my favorite. His words made me feel like I was sitting in front of one of those good guy, bad guy videos.

Yeah, all right, sure. I'd rather die with your knife up my gizzard, while you eat my eyeballs and then cut off my head, just after you neuter me with a rusty butter knife, of course. Yep. Sounds like a total ball.

"You can kiss my white-boy ass. That ain't ever going to happen. We're going to take you out, got me?" said a voice that sounded surprisingly like mine.

Wait. It *was* me.

"I must agree with the seer," said Arzur.

"You can kiss my blue ass as well," said Sabrea, laughing magically.

I love this woman.

"Have it your way, Triad."

The fight began so quickly that I barely had time to raise my arm before Arzur and Sabrea had reached the crest of the hill.

Two heads flew in, performing triple flips midair, while green blood sprang from sliced arteries, making interesting patterns in the sand.

Arzur flashed again and then stood in the midst of the surviving attackers, hands a complete blur, the loud reports of clanging metal disrupting the air as he fought two would-be executioners at once.

On the other side, two more Culroids had tumbled to the sand and down the slope, with those odd metal arrows protruding from various locations in their throats. Another rolled to a lurching stop, his head resting on the toes of my boot, one arrow firmly lodged between the low slung eye and the twisted nose of this attacker who had tasted Sabrea's wrath.

I quickly pulled my foot away, staring at the almost lifeless creature who had wanted to separate my heart from body. His mouth opened to speak, his hand reaching for me, but I sensed no threat. Inexplicably, I felt an almost overwhelming pang of compassion. Without a doubt, this seer insight had reached deep at this moment of death and spoke to me.

He hadn't always been this monster; this pariah of evil had another existence before this one. At least that was my impression. He'd been far nobler, far more benevolent, even kind in a different place in time. I almost wanted to touch him, to comfort him as he left this life.

Let's just take another drink from the fountain of *I just don't get it.*

In the next second, I glanced up and saw that the leader, the one who had spoken to us, had dropped to his knees, reaching over his shoulder, as the soldiers on each side of him fought savagely to protect him.

He'd have to hurry with his plans though. Three more of his soldiers left for the next life as Sabrea took them out with the strong thrust of her sword through their midsections, coming out the other side, spilling entrails on the sand. Odd entrails at that. I'd never seen green and black guts in my life. Not even the road kill back home looked this bad. Never mind the immediate foreboding stench that combined with the initial odor of the Culroids. I thought skunks were unpleasant.

Arzur's approach to battle had changed. He'd dropped his sword and gone to hand-to-hand as he lifted two of them from the sand with two of his arms, snapping their necks with the other set of arms. My perception of his strength had been wrong. He was clearly raising over six-hundred pounds of dead weight off the ground and wasn't breaking a sweat, holding them high, admiring his handiwork.

My two friends were now converging on Captain Culroid, the one who'd spoken to us with deadly intent, but I suspected they might be a fraction late and I might be on my own.

The narrow, black metal blade, complete with an enlarged sighting device and odd triggering mechanism underneath, had found its way into the leader's hands, and he quickly leveled the glowing weapon at my chest. The burst saber looked small, but I'd already seen what it could do. This thing had potential for a disastrous effect on my complexion.

His aura intensified into a bright black, if that were possible, as the crooked smile spread over his twisted features.

"Now you will die, Seer, white-boy ass and all," he said.

Our eyes met and . . . I saw it.

The hesitation, a split second of uncertainty that caused his mind to reset its intention, was as obvious as the weapon he held.

In that moment, I perceived his name. Molek. His name was Molek. And that wasn't all. He wasn't from Sabrea's world. He'd somehow been altered from a far different creation into what was before me, confirming my insight to his dead comrade near my feet.

That change had been excruciating to withstand. He'd endured torture, sleep deprivation, pitch-black confinement, scourging, groin branding, and worst of all, the death of his loved ones and companions. He had fought the good fight against the force, but lost.

I was beginning to grow a new respect for the term *too much information.*

That glimpse into his psyche was only for a split second, but it was enough for me. I knew what I had to do next. Of course, if I was wrong, I'd look like the Thanksgiving turkey old Aunt Martha had over-baked by a couple of hours.

Charred had been the new golden brown for her.

Molek's finger began to pressure the trigger, even as he subconsciously fought his compelling internal directive to fry me.

Without reluctance, I raised the sword and hurled it with all of my might. I watched as it, surprisingly, headed in the general direction that I intended.

14-CHAPTER

Molek's expression of surprise, if you can really call a face like his revealing any true emotion, was intensely gratifying to me. Maybe not as much as the resounding clang of my version of a Tyrfing striking the burst saber head on, dislodging it from his hands and sending it to the sand. All in all, it has a great toss, if I say so myself.

The saber split into two distinct pieces beginning at the barrel. As it did, it released a jolt of energy toward the ground, resembling a spreading, miniature, red lightning bolt, and then lay ominously dark. My rapier did not fall flat, but did something entirely different, as if given a command.

The sword stood erect, blade in the sand, hilt reflecting soft light from a now setting sun, mere feet from Molek. The man-monster eyed it, yet he made no attempt to reach for it.

This large creature would most certainly be a near match for Arzur and Sabrea, and me, if he'd chosen that route. He didn't. More odd behavior to ponder.

"Let us finish this," said Arzur as he reached our would-be destroyer.

"Agreed," said Sabrea, raising her crossbow.

"No!" I yelled. "No!"

Arzur's quick look of consternation rivaled Sabrea's but she grasped my intention before he did and reached out to grip his shoulder.

"Wait," she said.

"Why? He must die. He will be one less harbinger of death to combat our cause."

Great word, harbinger. But I didn't think Molek was a harbinger by choice. I was beginning to receive a vison of the Master and how he operated, even if I hadn't grasped the whole picture yet. That could be denial on my part, I suppose.

Hell, it probably was. I'd have to sort that out too.

"There is time enough for that, Arzur, if we need to go there. Just give me a minute," I said.

The quality of my voice had changed. It was calm, persuasive, and sort of sexy too. I need to bottle this one for when I get home to Kara. It could be a great night or two.

Kara's face suddenly shot across my mind's eye. She was the most wonderful woman on the planet, and God in heaven, I loved her far beyond what I'd realized.

It occurred to me, as I dealt with missing her, that I might never see her again. Never feel her lips on mine or touch the curve of her face or make love into the early morning, enjoying every moment of that intimacy. Never have Apollo lick my face sideways again.

How was I going to get home? I didn't even know how to begin that journey.

Shaking my head, I dismissed those thoughts for the time being. I had to. There's an old saying about living in the present so you can see tomorrow. I needed to do that.

"Are you well, Seer?" Arzur asked, tilting his massive, bearded head.

"I am. Just too many things running around in my brain."

Continuing my stroll up the dune, I stood above Molek, who hadn't bothered to look up as I arrived. It was as if he was, dare I say it, ashamed. Oddly enough, his aura was completely gone.

I fell to my knees and waited for him. Slowly, like one of those huge overhead doors, he lifted his head, searching my face.

My heart jumped, literally, as I saw the tears roll down those pocked cheeks.

Sabrea exhaled while Arzur only grunted. I took both reactions as surprise, relatively sure neither had ever seen a Culroid cry.

"I've killed dozens of seers, but none such as you. Who *are* you?" Molek whispered.

You know, under these bizarre circumstances, that was becoming an extremely legitimate enquiry. I decided to shelf that too, for now.

Man, my next session of quiet time was going to be anything but. The longer I belonged to this situation, the more unanswered questions arose . . . and still no barmaid in sight.

I put my hand on his strong arm. He flinched and began to pull his arm away, then stopped.

"The better question is who are you, Molek? You were ready to kill me and stopped. Why?"

He shook his head. "You know my name, and I yours, Gabriel. But I don't know why I stopped. I can only say that the moment you touched my mind, my thoughts rushed toward a different place in time for me. When I was not doing the bidding of the Master and—"

Molek's stare was a distant one as he looked past me. You know the kind that we all do when we're remembering or contemplating some significant event.

"And what?"

". . . and I was free to do as I pleased. When I knew nothing of this battle for the realms and cared even less that there was such a thing as good and evil. Right and wrong. Horrible deaths and eternal consequences."

Standing slowly, Arzur's sword a foot from his back, Molek straightened to his full six and a half feet, fingering his face with both hands as he did.

"Before my appearance was such," he said so softly that I barely heard him.

Tilting toward me, he offered his version of a frown with the one long eyebrow over his larger eye slanting downward.

Yep. Just like Sloth.

"Again, Gabriel, I've not encountered a seer like you. Who are you and where do you come from?"

I smiled. "From Earth, Molek."

He smiled back, I think. "Ahh. Of course you are. Which realm, Seer?"

"We don't exactly trust you. We're not even on a first-name, let's-have-a-beer basis, you know. There's that whole burst saber incident to consider, so I'll wait before we get to talking about realms."

Yet, I knew we would be allies at the very least, and soon. Whatever mad mind initiated the hell he'd been dragged through had failed in its purpose here. The spark of who Molek truly was hadn't died.

His mysterious master had missed totally converting him, or Molek had somehow managed to conceal that spark so deeply that neither one of them realized it was there.

Either way, it was sort of nifty to have the seer gift bring him back to some semblance of sociable. I gave myself a gold star.

We still needed to work on his personal hygiene, however.

"I don't know about other seers. I don't even know about me so much, to answer your question. I only know there are times that this gift gives more than it takes, and I get to connect inside the minds of folks and see who they might truly be," I said.

"And that connection, as you say, causes a deep awareness of long-lost images in others?" asked Molek.

"It has for some, but nothing as dramatic as with you. Molek, do you remember the details of what I saw the moment we connected?"

Our captive nodded. "Only a few images for now. I am not sure I could see more and not take my life."

"Take your life?"

Molek exhaled. "I've been freed from that slavery by whatever magical touch you might possess. I'll not journey there again, Gabriel."

He carried the look of a kid who had awakened from a bad dream and was now tucked firmly between mom and dad with no intention of ever returning to his own bed.

My new blue friend stepped closer to the three of us, her fuchsia eyes alive. "We can continue this discussion and decide what to do with that Culroid at a later point. We must go before another problem arises. An even bigger one, perhaps," said Sabrea.

"Problem? I don't see no stinkin' problem," I answered, grinning.

"You have such an odd sense of hilarity," said Arzur, frowning.

"Indeed," said Sabrea. "But I find it refreshing, in a human sort of way."

"Human? Is that good?"

"Ahh, we shall see, Gabriel," she answered, flashing a wide smile.

"She is correct," said Molek. "The Master is aware of your Triad and is anxious to see you destroyed."

"Why just us? Are there no other Triads?" asked Sabrea.

"There is but one other than yours. The Master's focus is not there, however. I believe he deems you more worthy of his attention."

Looking around at the dead Culroids, I didn't want any more of his attention for now.

I was about to ask Sabrea to lead the way, when without warning, my brain was abruptly on fire. I hit the sandy deck, unable to control my legs, as if they no longer belonged to me.

As a kid, I had accidently stepped on hot charcoal ashes that had been dumped outside of our campsite during a summer vacation. My foot was wrapped for a couple of weeks, and the blisters had been totally brilliant. The scars even more excellent, in terms of showing one's battle wounds.

The invasion in my mind felt like those same hot embers, only on the inside.

Without thinking, I threw up my best mental guard and felt the searing agony diminish so that I could gather some focus, but the pain was still whispering to me.

At the same moment in time, I received a strange vision in which I watched as Arzur, Sabrea, and Molek all reached for me, trying to rescue me from the sandy ground, which was sure to leave gritty grains in my underwear and subsequently in my nether parts. But they were unsuccessful, and all of them were sent plunging through space, landing some fifteen feet from me, puzzled expressions on their faces.

Then he was there.

In the middle of my soul, it seemed, stood the being I knew instinctively as the Master. His red cloak flowed from his hooded head to cover the full length of his seven-foot frame, hiding his face and eyes. His upright posture told me he was powerful and arrogant.

Not a pretty combination for the good guys.

Standing, I sensed I wasn't really in the desert, but hadn't truly left either. I was somewhere between that reality and one held tightly by this evil incarnate, a place where he was in total control.

"Gabriel Andrew Stark. It is a *pleasure* to meet you," said the Master.

More surprises. This being's voice was female. And she and "pleasure" were the most intimate of friends, just not the kind of pleasure you and I might enjoy. Unless you're a total sadist. Her knowledge and indulgence of the expansive and uninhibited concepts regarding torment were immense. A chill scurried up and down my spine.

Mustering my limited bravado, I addressed her. "I wish I could say the same. Who the hell are you and why am I here?"

"Those are questions you seem to ponder often, Gabriel."

She had me there.

"I've never lost a leg before, been exposed to auras, met a guy in a white tux who disappeared at will, spoke to someone who said they were my other mother, been attacked by a four-armed giant, walked through a gateway into another world that was the same as Earth only different, and battled some really ugly dudes side by side with a blue woman and another four-armed giant. Oh yeah. And entered the mind of one of my attackers, which led me to you. So forgive me if I ask a few questions, okay?"

I was seething.

She laughed, but as she did, at least for a moment, I sensed some unease within my hostess, or whatever she was. Her recovery was so rapid and complete that I wondered if I'd really sensed anything at all.

"I do understand, Gabriel. It must all seem so, unreal. As if you are in a dream, yes?"

Had me again.

"Yes. But this isn't some drug-encouraged state, I'm sure of that."

"Are you?"

I didn't answer. Hell no, I wasn't, now that we mention it again.

She walked toward me, head down, hands clasped together, hidden by the long sleeves of her spotless cloak.

"You are in the midst of a deep hallucination, Gabriel. There is no other realm involving Earth. There are no seers, warriors, or navigators let alone a Triad. There is no Samuel. And you have only one mother. You are not in the midst of some eternal battle between good and evil. Do you really think you could vanquish a creature such as Trench? All of this is a figment of your imagination and effects from a powerful pain medication regimen."

"Really? Says who? I mean, the fact that I'm talking to a seven-foot woman who won't show me her face lends less validity to reality than your contradicting words."

Spoken like a true bill collector. I still had it. Now I just needed her to say the check was in the mail.

I sounded confident, but the truth is, I wasn't. In fact, my mind was already running with the hopeful possibility that I was truly hallucinating. If that were true, it would mean I'd leave this mind-bending world and would eventually wake up and see Kara again. That was a reality that I could live with.

Her hands separated and reached for the hood that enigmatically concealed her face.

"You dwell on Kara. She is most certainly the center of your existence. Is that not true?" she asked, both of her long, beautiful hands still gripping the sides of her hood.

Good question. Without her and our big black Lab, I didn't see many more relationships that mattered to me. My little brother Luke and Dave Wymer were about it after that. Center of my existence? Yeah, that's correct.

"That's not a secret," I said. Odd. My voice took on characteristics of some subtle echo chamber. I didn't know how, but my environment, this Never-Never Land, was altering in a way I couldn't perceive. Like I was traveling far away without moving.

"No, for most, the love of our lives is not something that can be hidden. It is as it should be. Would you die for her, Gabriel?"

"That's a dumbass question, of course."

"Truly?"

"Yes."

"Then would you also live for her?"

"What does that mean?"

She didn't answer. Instead, slowly, like some dancer in a tantalizing tease show (not that I've seen one, mind you), she pulled the hood away from her face.

This world immediately began to spin out of control as the woman's hands and features began to melt, turning to a crimson liquid, but not before I recognized her face. How could I not?

The image of my lovely wife Kara had been hidden under that cloak.

15-CHAPTER

There wasn't really a sense of flipping through any time-space continuum, if I even understood what that meant. This most perplexing journey to consciousness, and returning to my hospital bed, was more like driving through a spiraled racetrack in a complete fog and then, at the very last turn, having the sunlight break through that pea soup so brilliantly that you were almost blinded. That's my best shot at any explanation of being pitched into the hospital bed.

At any rate, I awoke to the din of excited activity and a room so filled with dazzling auras that I immediately slammed my eyes shut.

As realization crawled its fickle path to my senses, I instinctively concentrated on dimming the wattage of those auras. I could sense that it had worked.

When I reopened my eyes, I could see the collective auras were under control, but the mass of medical personnel hadn't done the light fandango out of my room.

Dr. Thomas, Kara, and a nurse and two orderlies I didn't recognize were hovering over me like mother hens protecting their chicks from a slick weasel. (Hey, I'm an old farm boy.)

Talk about a reality check. Only moments before, it seemed, I'd been talking to a seven-foot woman wearing a red cloak who was the spitting image of my wife, and who I thought was the essence of evil as the Master. Previous to that, I'd been developing a rapport with some ugly, deformed, hell-bent-on-death cuss. Now, here I was, back in a bed that I'd apparently never left.

Are dreams that take on this type of deep-seated veracity common? It was like dreaming you had to pee and then woke up just in time to make it to the john. Except deeper. And what of the auras? There was no denying them. Was there? Could they simply exist as a symptom of the accident, and it was taking my eyes longer to adjust to instant light when I awoke?

I don't know. I don't know. Did I?

Moving my eyes around the room, I landed on the good doctor and asked the big question again. "What's going on?"

"We be checkin'," said Dr. Thomas.

"Did I die? Did I OD on chocolate?"

"No, Gabe. It be sometin' else. But I didn't tink of the chocolate ting. We're just tryin to figure ya out," she said.

"Figure me out?"

"Ya. Why are ya like you are now?"

Samuel's *Three Musketeers* imitation immediately came to mind, and I quickly reached for my abdomen with, uncannily, not even a crease of pain in my midsection or my right arm. Hell, I had no pain anywhere.

Moving my hand back and forth over my midsection, I searched for a deep crevice that should have allowed my entrails to unravel somewhere beside my hip. There should have been a messy clump of guts. Nothing.

How could that be? I should have been a poster child for men in white tuxes not playing with long, sharp swords in hospital rooms. Let's not even consider my whole trip to Sabrea's realm.

Damn. It was unsettling to refer to someone in a dream by her name. I thought my days of make-believe friends had evaporated with age. Of course, I am male. We never quite get that growing-up thing.

So what was the truth here?

I told you I could be a bit slow on the uptake sometimes, but it seemed, as of right now, my strange visitor just might be someone close to who he said he was. Or, the more probable explanation, I had been hallucinating to a degree that would make the sixties crowd proud.

It's my red hair, isn't it?

Have I mentioned my desire for hard cider?

By now the staff had grown eerily quiet. It reminded me of the silent mortification you feel when you're gossiping about someone—ohhh, say, a boss—who is suddenly standing a few feet behind you, having heard every disparaging word. It happened to a friend once. Not me, a friend. I stopped groping myself, gazed around the room, and waited for someone to speak. No one did. But I remained the subject of everyone's curious stare; even the unflappable Dr. Thomas was quiet.

"What?" I said finally, with more energy than I thought I possessed.

I was still feeling—great. No pain anywhere. I felt so much better than the last time I subsisted among the conscious. The wonders of modern medicine are truly amazing, aren't they? Or . . . No. No no no. There is no Samuel or any other fairytale here. It's in my head.

Kara then entered the room and adopted a seat beside me, flashing a bewildered, grateful look. She leaned forward. The subtle scent of her natural fragrance drifted to my nose. It registered in me just how much I loved everything about her.

Everything. Hadn't I just confessed that to my red-cloaked confidant? Stop. She wasn't real.

Kara touched my arm gently. "Gabe, twelve minutes ago, at twelve minutes after five, all your monitors flat-lined. We thought that you . . . you had checked out again. When the crew rushed in, well, all of your monitors, IVs, and feeding tubes had been disconnected from your body. Gabe, honey, you were out like a light, but very much alive."

"How can that happen?" I asked with obvious doubt.

"We don't know. You may have been able to pull one or two of them out, but no way could you have removed everything. It just wasn't possible."

The love of my life glanced back to Dr. Thomas, and I saw the slight nod directed toward Kara.

"Was there anyone . . . did anyone else come into the room, anything like that?"

For reasons unknown to me at the time and unvarnished later, I intuitively shot a searching look directly at Dr. Thomas. She was boring into me with dark, purposeful eyes and seemed to have an almost preternatural interest in any answer I might offer.

There was more.

I abruptly recalled not seeing an aura around her when she had introduced herself originally. That train was now derailed. I captured the faintest of outlines about her, except it really wasn't light, but more succinctly, the absence of light. Perhaps a mini black hole would best serve as a model here. Then it disappeared.

I shivered.

Put that in my reality pipe and smoke it. Bad eyes? I don't think so.

No matter how fleeting a glimpse I had partaken of during my first encounter with black auras, the experience was firmly and indelibly etched in my mind, indeed my very soul. I regained my composure and knew one thing for certain: until I could figure out what the hell was going on here, there would be no mention of my new friend Samuel. For one of the few times in my life, I felt compelled to lie. I hated lying, but, for a plethora of reasons, I deemed it the right thing to do.

"I didn't see anyone," I said, still looking at the good doctor. "Besides, don't you monitor the comings and goings of anyone entering the floor?"

"Dat's true," she said, in her best bedside manner voice. "No one saw anything and so far dere is nothin' outta da ordinary from da cameras, but we still be lookin'."

The room repeated the silent act. I looked away from the doctor back to Kara.

"What difference does it make? I'm okay, right?"

My wife's stare was beginning to unnerve me. I felt like I had just been arrested for streaking, again.

She began her answer by bending to the floor then showing me the objects she had retrieved.

My mouth fell open. I needed to cultivate a new reaction to surprise. Although peeing my pants didn't seem to fit as a more viable solution.

"More than okay," she whispered.

Clenched tightly in her hands were the split-apart plaster casts that should have been embracing my left arm and left leg. I hadn't even realized I didn't have them on me. "All of your broken bones have, ah, seemed to have . . . mended. There doesn't appear to be any fractures. Anywhere."

My wife was moving her head in that way people do when something just doesn't make a lick of sense, not taking her eyes from me.

"It isn't logical, but it's true," said Kara.

I stared at her like the quintessential deer in headlights. "Healed? Completely?"

"Yes. And there's more."

Kara leaned over the bed's aluminum railing and pulled back the ashen sheet covering my lower body. No, the leg had not returned from the land of lost limbs, but the area just above my knee flashed a completely healed stump. The skin was as vital and natural looking as the upper part of my leg.

"Can you explain any dis, Gabriel?" asked the doctor, her eyes narrowing in scrutiny.

"What kind of question is that? Hell no, I can't explain it. How would I even have a clue? Other than Jesus returning just for me, and that doesn't seem to fit with my brother Luke's theology."

"Dat might be true, Gabriel. So what teology does fit here?" she asked.

I mentally pinched myself. I was alive and in the here-and-now. I was conscious. I was in the presence of these people. I felt the bed sheets against my bum, the touch of my wife's hands. The sterile scent of the hospital itself was palatable. Even the faces of the people and their incredulous expressions, right up to the squinting eyes and frowning foreheads were real. Very real. All of it.

Of course, the only plausible explanation was obvious, even to me. Samuel's blade hadn't divorced my torso from my legs, but instead had somehow healed me. That meant that he was real.

That meant the realm I'd visited and then subsequently left had been substantive. Not a figment of my deep imagination at all, but real. Sabrea and Arzur and Molek were not subconscious creations waltzing around in a dream world. Again, real. What of the mysterious Master?

For perhaps the very first time, I was forced to accept that this other realm, this other reality had validity and that I had a true purpose there. This realization spawned further questions that had to be addressed.

"What is it, Gabe?" asked Kara, interrupting my thoughts.

I slowly shook my head. "I just don't get it, that's all."

My eyes darted around the room. I was searching for the gotcha.

Dr. Thomas's eyes narrowed as she spoke. Her tone emanated a cool quality that seemed to belie her natural, carefree demeanor; like she was struggling to control intense emotion.

"Get it indeed, Gabriel. Dere are many documented cases of spontaneous regeneration, or healing, and I may have seen one or two. Dey are always soft-tissue healings, never bone. Dose folks who do da quantum-touch terapy claim dis kinda ting, but never on dis level." She frowned and searched for the proper words. "You saw no one, right?"

"No one. But If I had, who could do this, other than, like say, Jesus or maybe Yoda?"

She didn't smile and that made me more uncomfortable. I don't know how I knew, but she had knowledge of exactly what had transpired. I was just as convinced that she cared very little for it. Fear?

"It appears, Mr. Stark, you will be one for da medical journals," she iced.

My heart leapt as the physician's unsettling blackness flaunted another brief—and I suspected, intentional—appearance. I was beginning to get a sense that she could control her aura, or counter-aura, if you will.

I shivered again.

"I tink you will be da subject of great scrutiny, yes?"

I didn't think this scrutiny was going to be akin to a tropical vacation. And, if I had my way, I wouldn't be here to indulge anyone's curiosity.

16-CHAPTER

"Please leave. All of you. I need some time alone, all right?"

My plea sounded real. Mournful and pathetic, I must admit. But I had to think through this line of events and develop a plan to get out of this bed and go home.

"Even me, Gabe?" asked Kara, those big eyes nearly breaking my heart, but I needed to figure this out and what to do if I did. She would only be a distraction to me. A pleasant one, as usual, but a distraction nevertheless. I had to admit, on top of that, I felt an uneasy anxiety with her remaining in the room. Was she in danger? Perhaps. I didn't know, but that felt right.

"Yes, honey, at least for a while. I have to deal with this."

"I understand. I'll be outside when you need me."

She kissed me, and her aura brightened noticeably as she walked out. Her aura was vivid and filled with love. No man had ever been loved by a better woman. I would always need her. Always—whatever that actually meant. Even the simplest of definitions seemed to elude me lately. I felt myself becoming pissy and impatient. The paradox of having her go and the others not taking her lead was flat-out annoying. Ever notice how medical folks think the rules don't apply to them?

"The rest of you can go now. Please just leave. Now."

Despite some more minor objections, they all finally relented. Dr. Thomas was the last to leave.

Bending close, she whispered. "I be around too, Gabriel. I be around. We shall see what we see, ya?"

"Just leave."

She did, and for whatever reason—one she controlled, I'd bet—that unnerving black aura didn't reappear as she sauntered toward the door, throwing one last look my way conveying that she would be watching me. I didn't doubt it.

Hey, *I* was going to be watching me.

I removed the comforter and stared at the healed stub on my leg. Why not give me the complete leg? It would have been just as easy for

Samuel to do that, I suspected. Yet, I thought I knew why.

Maybe restoring the leg was out of reach or all part of the plan. Could be either. Perhaps regenerating a limb was too far down the spontaneous healing road to be accepted by anyone in the medical world, or by laymen either, for that matter. That kind of thing just doesn't happen, and in case you didn't realize, we live on a very small planet these days. Word of such a thing would be around the world in hours. I would be the subject of countless interviews, tests, theories, demon exorcisms . . . people would literally want a piece of my booty.

I read a lot and knew that there are rare, but not unheard of, situations of miraculous spontaneous healings documented worldwide. I had not, however, read of unprompted limb regeneration for humans. That mysterious ability seemed restricted to salamanders and such. As miraculous as my healing appeared to be, it wasn't totally out of the world of possibilities and would draw less attention.

Okay. I could buy that. I *did* buy that.

And if I could buy into miraculous healing, then I could buy the rest of this journey too. And I did.

"Either it is or isn't, Gabe," I whispered.

When I was in high school, I enjoyed science classes because I believed those teachings a forum for proving theories, setting principles that I could follow the rest of my life. Proof was always better than theory for me, thus leading to the agnostic approach I adopted regarding God's existence, much to the chagrin of my pastor brother, Luke.

At any rate, Mr. Bridges in physics class introduced me to the principle of Occam's razor. He explained it like this: "When you have two competing theories that make exactly the same predictions, the simpler one is the better."

That's where I was.

Spontaneous healing that just happened to coincide with my dreams of other realms, yada, yada, yada, didn't fit nearly as neatly as the one where I actually *saw* Samuel raise his sword, healing me, and sending me to the next world.

I know. I know. But that line of thinking is far more feasible. After all, I am healed, bones included. I even had a sweet new mechanical leg that helped me to learn to walk incredibly quickly.

Reaching my hand to touch the leg, I wondered where the prostheses had gone. The leg that had sent Trench to his death had been real. I'd felt it. Mother Mary had tested it. Even though I still have no idea where it came from, it was mine.

I think I know why it isn't here. If that would have crossed realms with me . . . well, try 'splaining that one, Lucy.

Obviously, I wouldn't have been able to explain it. That fact opened up more questions about traveling back and forth between Sabrea's world and mine (that sounds so *Twilight Zone*) that would surely make my head hurt.

Like for starters, how does that work—this realm-traveling stuff—and who sets that principle in place? Does anyone? Is it simply a matter of knowledge or does Samuel open that door? Or is this all orchestrated by . . . well, by God or something related to that concept? What role did that Master chick hold? Obviously she had dug into my thoughts and pulled Kara's image, voice, and mannerisms to entice me to want to go home, but to what end? She said there was no reality where I was concerned. That it was all a dream, yet I'm healed in this real world in an unreal way.

Headache number twenty-nine was rolling down the track, and I needed medication. How was I supposed to figure this all out?

"You have the answers, Gabriel."

I jumped as I found my favorite purple-eyed sword swinger staring at me from his usual spot at the foot of the bed.

"Samuel! You have to stop doing that. I hate being—"

I stopped, the look on his pale face causing me to catch my smartass response. He was in pain, but I couldn't tell which kind, physical or mental. I found myself, out of nowhere, wanting it to be physical because I believed he could heal himself or something akin to what he'd done for me. Mental anguish, on the other hand, isn't always so easily mended.

I sat up on my elbows. "Are you all right? You look like crap."

His smile was slow and drawn out, as if he were contemplating the note of distress in my voice and had been struck with an epiphany. "Why, Gabriel, are you concerned with my wellbeing?"

"Good question. I suppose I am, since I've finally bought into the idea this world you introduced me to is authentic."

"Undeniably it is." The smile faded. "And what do you mean *look like crap*? I assure you, I never look like human excrement. That is extremely distasteful to consider."

My turn to smile. This boy needs to get out more.

"It's a figure of speech. It's not literal. I only meant you don't look like your normal self."

"Ahh. I see. You humans are a puzzle at times, even for me."

"I can see that. So?"

"So what?"

"What's wrong with you and why are you here?"

With a sudden, lightning-fast move, he clutched the railing at the foot of the bed, closing his eyes as he swayed to one side, his knees buckling.

I thought Samuel was going down for the count as I threw the covers off from me and started to get out of bed.

Oh, wait. No lower leg, remember?

I looked up, helpless and angry at the same time, but then he steadied himself, grasping the hilt of his sword like a knight of old as he stood tall.

"I am fine, Seer. Yet, others are not; they suffer. Those atrocious feelings sometimes reach me, and I must control my reaction to the plight of their pain," he explained, a shade paler now, despite his bravado.

I felt myself gazing past my leg and studying the floor, studying the cracks between the gray tiles. I could never get them that clean at home. I wonder what they use to keep them so sparkly?

At any rate, I knew precisely what he meant. The empathy could be every bit as encompassing as the tell-tale auras.

I was then thrust into the midst of an epiphany of my own.

How did Samuel seem to know when to show up? And why was he exhibiting the same seer rationality that I have? I knew the answers as quickly as the questions came.

"You're a seer, aren't you?" I said quietly.

That inscrutable gaze never wavered. "I know the gift well, Gabriel. But not the way you shall."

"You always talk in riddles to me. I feel like I'm on a game show. Tell me what—"

"Enough, Gabriel. I've come to help you find the answers to your questions, answers that have always dwelt within you."

I felt his urgency, or maybe it was impatience. And he was right; too many unanswered questions that really weren't. "Okay. Fair enough. What did you mean by I had the answers?"

"Often common sense is a graceful power on its own volition, Gabriel. What does your perception and deduction tell you?"

Another good question.

The answer was immediate. Kind of like closing your eyes before you hit the pool, diving from the ten-foot board. You were going to get wet the second you stepped on the gritty surface of the diving apparatus. One simply had to go through the steps, all of the while knowing the result.

Before Samuel had spoken, I knew what needed to transpire, but it wasn't something I truly wanted to do. I wanted to get out and go home, to be with Kara and Apollo, to get ready for Christmas.

I was most certainly going to leave this hospital bed, no question about that, but that act didn't include a trip to the old farmstead. Hardly. There was something more important here. I was going to miss making that batch of miracle fudge.

Exhaling, I stayed sitting on the edge of the bed facing Samuel, his gaze piercing and deep. I could see his pain, but his expectations of me were undeniably stronger than anything he was experiencing. He was sort of like the dad watching to see if his son would do the right thing and not pull the wings off the fly firmly secured between his chubby fingers.

No wing-pulling for me today. I had other things to do.

It's funny how the pressure of doing the right thing is alleviated when you make up your mind to do it, no matter the repercussions.

Leaning closer to him, my voice grew softer for reasons I can't quite comprehend other than the softness led to a growing determination and conviction in my heart of hearts. "I never thought I'd say this, but I need to get back to Sabrea and Arzur."

"Why?"

"First because I am not at all sure that realm is real. I mean, who would think so?"

"And?"

And was right. The embers of anger began to grow inside of me as I contemplated the other true reason I had to go back. My mom used to say anger was unbecoming. I say anything, in the right circumstance, is becoming, including the emotion building in me now. Ever heard of righteous anger?

My voice grew even calmer. "Because I think that red-caped wench wanted me gone so she could destroy our Triad. To derail whatever we had going. I think they need me and—"

Hesitating, I had another revelation. Good God, I relished being an easygoing, loveable kind of guy. Life was far less complex when we get to stay where we are totally comfortable. But that wouldn't do here. I was thinking of Sabrea and Arzur and Molek, but I was thinking of something far nobler as well.

I found myself compelled to stand up and fight for what was right. I'd seen the effects of unchecked evil in the faces and actions of the Culroids and the unveiled deception and intent of the Master's thoughts and actions. I'd seen auras laced with unequivocal goodness, and I'd seen the black outlines that had made me shiver and want to hide under the covers. Which wasn't a bad idea now. Because I was getting a little chilly thanks to the infamous hospital gown, which was not exactly covering everything that needed to be covered.

Pulling the sheet over my shoulders, I searched his face. "Samuel. I get it. This is my fight, and I was chosen—or whatever this destiny stuff truly means—to take the fight to a different level."

"Well said, Seer. Go you must," he said putting his hand on my shoulder.

"Okay. Let's do it. Hit me with that sword of yours. But can you make it less painful? Last time it hurt like crazy and—"

He was staring at me again.

"What?"

"You have to travel on your own this time, Gabriel."

"You know, you're not making this easy. Just how do I do that?"

"You simply have to will it. You are much more equipped than you realize. Concentrate."

"You mean like Christopher Reeves in *Somewhere in Time*?" (Don't laugh. I love that movie.)

"I don't know of what you speak, but you have the power. Use it."

Once again, he was right. I *did* have the ability. I felt it. Yet focus wasn't always my best attribute.

"Okay," I answered, doubt getting the best of me. Sometimes knowledge isn't enough. It's what one does with it.

So, like all people not wanting to fail, I stalled. "Oh, one more question. What will the staff and my wife think when I'm gone?"

"Gabriel. What did they think when you were gone the first time?"

"Oh, got it."

"It is time. You must hurry, Seer. You dawdle."

"Hey, I've never dawdled in my life."

Squeezing my eyes tight I began to concentrate on . . . well, what was it I was supposed to be concentrating on? I saw Kara's face in the deception of the Master, her red hood concealing something far more sinister. I thought about Mother Mary, then was struck with a desire to see my true mother, and suddenly wanted a piece of her to-die-for cherry pie. Throw a little French vanilla ice cream on that, and who cares about another heaven?

Strange what enters our minds when we least expect it. Comfort food from my mother? A sure-fire sign that stress and I were hanging out again. Then I heard it. Subtle, but effective, and just for me.

Focus, Seer. Many lives depend on it.

The thought rushed into my mind and then out again. Samuel was indeed a talented creation. I girded my mental loins, interesting thought, and did what I felt compelled to do; concentrate on something other than me.

"I've got this," I whispered.

Closing my eyes, I concentrated on Arzur and Sabrea. Their thoughts, their auras, their surroundings.

Slowly, the white sand came into blurred view in my mind's eye, and suddenly, I felt the desert breeze caressing my face. I was once again engulfed by that wonderful flowery scent and swore I could feel the gritty sand under my feet. More succinctly, under my now on-again boots.

I opened my eyes and watched the bed begin to dissipate. Miraculously the metal leg once again was attached below my knee.

The black britches covered my legs followed by the boots and then the shirt. This was undoubtedly the coolest way I'd ever gotten dressed. I fleetingly wondered what my underwear was like. A cotton blend? Silk? Boxers? Briefs?

My body began to vibrate, but in a calm, controlled way, and I knew I was almost there.

"Gabriel!"

Sabrea's rich voice confirmed it.

As the hospital room distorted and vanished, I wondered if I'd ever see it or Kara again for I knew that death and its strange emissaries were sprinting wildly in my direction.

17-CHAPTER

Perched on my elbows, I sat up as Arzur and Molek hovered a few feet away while Sabrea, kneeling to my left, broke into another of those magical smiles.

"What happened to you, Seer? Where did you go?" asked the four-armed giant.

Arzur's voice was unbroken, but I'll be hornswoggled if there wasn't a trace of concern.

"Could you be more specific please?" I asked.

"You just passed out and . . . well, it was like your body became transparent for a brief moment. Then you returned, wide awake," said Sabrea.

I frowned. "How long was I out?"

"Just moments, I suppose. The sun is in about the same position, so it was not long," she answered.

Remembering the clock in the hospital room, I realized that my journey to Sabrea's earth had only taken around fifteen minutes from Mother

Mary to my coerced return. I wasn't sure what the accelerated time lapse from one world to anther represented exactly. I perhaps had an idea or two, but like the details and other nuances of this journey, it would come to me eventually, like it or not.

Standing, I reached for Sabrea's hand, motioned for Arzur to come to me, and nodded at Molek. The circle closed around me as I moved from one face to another, auras moving to the brighter side of the light scale, vivifying my mind and cementing our thoughts at the same time.

Everyone in this circle needed to hear what I had to say. Even though I knew it would mean different things to each of them, they would understand. Wait. Maybe it was I who needed to speak to them more than they needed to listen.

"Listen. At first, I thought our meeting one another was simply some elaborate dream. Some terrible mind joke. Even when the Master spoke to me, taking on the persona of my wife, I thought it was a jumbled set of memories and desires making a perfect storm of common sense."

"The Master spoke to you?" asked Molek.

"She did."

He nodded, an attempt at a crooked grin accompanying that attempt. "You have given the Master reason for concern, Seer."

"Yeah. I'm getting that. That and another pep talk form Samuel have made me a believer in what's happening here."

Arzur drew close and put one of his hands on my shoulder.

I wonder what it costs to do a manicure on this guy.

Sabrea followed suit, putting her hand on Arzur's, her fuchsia eyes ablaze. Molek hesitated, raise his hand, and dropped it to his side, then with great effort and downcast eyes, put his large mitt on my other shoulder.

I put my hand over Molek's hairy paw. He wasn't part of the Triad, yet for some unknown reason, I now trusted him. The awareness of evil I'd experienced with the Master had given me a sense of awe on how Molek had kept his ember of decency hidden from that evil. He was going to be important here. I just knew it. And more than that, I sensed, the others knew it as well.

"All I want to say is that I'm in, completely. I believe in what we're called to do and will do my best to be what I'm called to be," I said.

Sabrea pushed away the hands of the males, lifted me from the sand, and licked my face, grinning as she set me back down. "I have love for you, Seer."

"That's how you show it? Licking my face?"

"Yes. My people find that lip-meeting gesture your people engage in a trifle rudimentary. Tongue on face is far more affectionate and pleasurable. Wouldn't you agree?"

"I'm not too sure about that, but, hey, when in Rome."

I got on my tiptoes and licked her cheek.

"Ohh, Gabriel. You are as talented a licker as you are a seer. I am getting very warm." She faked a swoon and then laughed as hard as I'd ever heard her.

That wondrous sound caused me to laugh as well. Arzur and Molek joined us with light laughs so I guess that was progress for them. I suspected any form of hilarity was something neither of them had enjoyed in a long while.

When the laughter faded, Molek pointed toward the sun. "I am humbled by your acceptance, but I think it is time to do as Sabrea suggested and find refuge. Your Triad must be completed."

"He is correct," agreed Sabrea.

Scanning the horizon in all directions I saw nothing except sand and the occasional clump of trees or vegetation.

"Okay, but I don't see anywhere to go," I said.

"Ahh. That, Seer, is why you need a navigator such as myself," replied Sabrea. "There is refuge not so far away."

"Lead on, then."

She began down the slope, stepping over two Culroid bodies. I followed.

"Wait."

I turned toward Arzur and saw that he was pointing in the direction we were headed.

"That direction will not do," he said.

It took a moment for me to see what Arzur saw.

At first, I thought I was just focusing on the horizon and the sand was simply meeting the sky to form a slight shadow. Then that massive shadow moved.

I felt the chill run down, then back up, my spine. It wasn't a shadow at all.

Culroids. Thousands of them.

"The soldiers of the Master are many," said Molek softly. "And they want you all dead."

18-CHAPTER

"Great God of life. We must go in this direction. It will take longer, but it is safe. Follow me," said Sabrea, pointing forty-five degrees away from the approaching horde.

Scrambling down the dune, we fell into line, Arzur bringing up the rear just behind Molek, who was directly behind me.

Sabrea broke into a run, and again I was surprised by the ease with which I followed. I didn't run much back home, maybe to the dinner table and back to the couch, and that was on a good night. Yet here I was, stride for stride with her, even with the sword bouncing on my left thigh. It was eerie that I was not breathing hard at all, even after a half hour at this pace.

I pulled up beside her, turned around, and began running backwards. "Hey, what do you think of this?"

"I think you are silly and need to be more serious," she said.

"What? That from the lady of jokes?"

"Oh yes. I also think you need to watch—"

I don't know if you've heard the term "ass over teakettle," but the next second, I was exactly that.

My right heel hit something hard, a rock maybe, and I was rolling like tumbleweed across the prairie in an old western. Then abruptly, I wasn't. Two strong hands righted me, and then I was just as quickly released from that grip.

"We run for our lives, and you play like a child. You are truly odd, Seer," said Arzur as he trotted ahead of me.

Brushing myself off, I glanced behind us. "Yeah, but I . . ."

The rest of my witty retort failed to make an appearance as I stood staring at the horizon. The horde was still coming, but I sensed that we had put a good bit of distance between us. What we hadn't considered, however, was how long it would take for them to eventually reach us, and by what means, and just how badly the Master wanted that to happen.

The dozens of tiny dots in the late afternoon sky were growing larger by the second. I found myself fascinated by the process. It sort of reminded me of the flying monkeys in the *Wizard of Oz.*

The other three drew up beside me, staring at the same phenomena that had my full attention.

"What are they, Molek?" I asked.

He shook his head. "I do not know exactly. They were talks of such creatures, but I have not encountered them."

"What talks?"

He touched his saber at his belt. "They were just gossip. Rumors."

"What talks, Molek?" I asked again.

"It is said that the Master would have need of winged beasts to conquer all three realms. That they were created by the Master's evil magic from other conquered races. Much like the Culroids."

There was more.

"And?"

Molek hesitated. It was odd to witness any sort of tentativeness for this former commander of the Culroids and bondservant of the Master. But I gathered that with each passing moment, his sense of nobility was returning, allowing for an entirely different take on his situation. Evil was losing its contemptible grip, and I, for one, found it quite encouraging.

"Molek?"

"And to destroy the remaining Triads before they joined the battle. Those Triads, like yours, would be powerful and a threat to his plans. The Master will stop at nothing to prevent that."

Arzur stepped forward. "So he would need a two-pronged attack to distract, attack, and kill," said Arzur. "It is a good battle strategy."

"Well, I don't want to be on the short end of this strategy," I said.

"That is wise, Seer. Whatever they are, they are making up distance quickly. We must hurry," said Sabrea.

I shot one last look at the growing spectacle in the sky and felt something I hadn't felt in a long while.

As a kid, I'd gotten into a fight or two, and my principle, Mr. Kirby, after one of his *wooden paddle across the ass to get my attention* sessions, had told me, "Son, you can't fight the entire world." He told me to lose the anger, even if I was not sure where it came from.

Over time, he'd said, it would come to me on what that anger was all about, but not to live my life searching for the source of my pissiness. He said it'd be a waste, and I'd be able to handle it later. I didn't get all of what he was referring to, but most of it. He was right, of course.

Yet, at this moment, as I turned to follow my three odd companions, for whom I'd built an appreciation, I had grown suddenly pissed. *Really* pissed.

It didn't take long for me to realize why either.

I was angry. Angry that we were the good guys and were running to save our fannies. Why does that always seem to be true? I mean, look what happened to Luke Skywalker.

Where was *my* Master? *My* helper? *My* horde? Hell, *my* flying legion against the antithesis of whatever cavernous pit of darkness those creatures had escaped?

I found it precipitously odd that I'd met the evil's leader but hadn't met the leader of the "forces of good," lacking a better analogy.

The odds against us would be hopeless if we chose to fight, even for warriors as talented as my assembly appeared to be.

I don't get it. Why does evil always carry the battle? Why can't we hit the path of aggression and kick some serious bad-boy ass with an army of our own? I mean, come on, who really wants the worshipers of darkness to triumph and rule? They first thing they'd do would be to shut down the beaches, then the Tiki bars, then the parasailing. Then everyone would have to wear black and don handcuffs and be transformed into some horrible version of the Culroids or whatever.

I didn't look that good in black, personally.

Assuming that every race on this earthly three-plane existence felt somewhat as I, we should be able to grow an even more magnificent army than the mass headed in our direction, right?

"Come, Seer. You may contemplate our potential leaders under a far more favorable set of circumstances, but for now, we need to get our asses in motion, as you would say," said Sabrea, wrapping her strong fingers around my arm.

Facing her, I saw her wonderful aura grow brighter. Almost as bright as her smile.

"I keep forgetting we're joined at the mind, sort of."

"Not completely joined, as you say, Gabriel, but I don't believe I need a mind link to read your thoughts while you stare at what darkness has gathered."

"I suppose that's true. Still, the question remains: why are we always up the underdog creek without a paddle for the canoe?"

She waved the question away, but I knew she had a question or two of her own.

"Later, Seer. Move your carcass."

I turned and began running with her.

"Carcass?"

"Yes. I find some of your human terms endearing. That is one of them."

"I'll see if I can find a couple more."

"I would like that."

"Do you know what a dickhead is?"

"I'll look forward to your colorful explanation, Seer. But we need to move faster."

"Deal."

We reached Arzur and Molek, some twenty yards in front of us and then broke into a semi-sprint, four across, sand flying behind us as we moved in a purposeful direction that only Sabrea seemed to understand.

Navigator indeed.

As we crested the next dune, I heard the sand explode some twenty feet behind us, startling the sin out of me.

Glancing back, I saw that the sky resembled a locust attack emulating one of the ten plagues directed by Moses to free the Israelites. Except these "locusts" were the size of grown women and carrying burst sabers and a shitty attitude.

"How did they get here so quickly?" I yelled, sprinting down the shaded side of the next dune, a few feet behind Sabrea.

I never heard a response from any of them, if there was one. Because the next instant, I experienced another sensation of hurtling through the air, my feet taken out from under me, twisting like an acrobat gone wrong, then more of that damned darkness.

19-CHAPTER

The thump I heard in that blackness, then subsequently experienced was . . . illuminating. I'd manage to twist to my left and then fall onto something both soft and hard. There was a brief moment of wondering if I'd ever catch another breath, followed by a well-thought-out string of obscenities that any New York wise guy would be proud of.

"Get off me, Seer," said Arzur.

I tried to respond and tell him I wasn't in his lap by choice, but nothing came out. It didn't matter. A moment later, I was off him anyway.

I felt three hands lift me and set me down a couple of feet from where I'd fallen, ass-first again, yet this time the thump wasn't so bad.

As I sat there, eyes shut, still struggling to find my breath, I lined up my contemplated response to Arzur's total lack of respect for my position as a seer.

Maybe.

I finally took in my first breath since the tumble from the surface. That wait for returning dislodged air can drag on for what seems like days. Not a good feeling on any level, but a total revelation when one is able to draw freely from one's lungs. It's the little things.

As I was learning to breathe again, I caught an odor in the air. Wherever we were had a similar smell to the dank, stale air of our Michigan basement back home, yet without the dampness that always accompanies that special stink.

Opening my eyes—and I had to make sure they were indeed open—all I could see was blackness. Perhaps the fall had crippled me in another way and that I was as blind as a liberal in church.

What a paradox that would be: a blind seer.

That line of thinking disappeared the very second I saw the fuchsia ovals to my left.

I leaned forward and reached out, touching someone, or something. "Sabrea?"

"Who else, Seer?"

"Your eyes are glowing."

"Yes. And what is your point?"

"Well, I wondered if they could belong to some strange underground dragon preparing to rip my arms off and use my bones for toothpicks, you know?"

Her eyes swung my way, leaving tracers of pink light in the wake of that turn.

"I assure you, Seer, there is no such creature in *this* place. And where you are touching me, while pleasant, should be explored at another time when we can be alone."

I yanked my hand back amidst her vivid laughter.

"Ahh, sorry."

"Apology accepted, Gabriel. You do have nice hands, however."

More laughter.

My face grew warmer, and I was thankful that no one could see me.

"Funny girl. So where are we?"

"A brief, but effective sanctuary," she said.

"Lights would help."

"One moment," said Molek from my right and a distance away.

"Indeed," said Arzur. "And where exactly were you touching her, Seer?"

"Really? You're asking me that?"

"I am."

"I'm not answering. The light, Molek?"

"I am working on it," he said.

A moment or two passed. Then just as the room began to lighten, I thought of a way to give us all a glimpse of where we were and what was around us. Maybe my version of the Vulcan mind meld could work here. Even though Sabrea had defined our location somewhat, I didn't have the feeling she was totally sure of what or where this place was. It wasn't necessary just yet, this method that had entered my mind, but you can bet your ass I filed it away for future reference.

The room grew gradually brighter, but it wasn't quite like turning on a light switch. It was more like a gradual unveiling. Kind of like the old Mercury lights we had on the barn and garage back home. Just flip on the switch and wait for what seemed like forever for them to warm up.

My dad had it down to a science and knew exactly when the natural light would leave for the day and when the artificial would kick in.

I ran my hand through my hair. Funny how that childhood memory came to me now, as some are wont to do in unusual circumstances, I suppose.

One thing was for sure, I couldn't think of many things weirder than the situation in which I was currently involved. Not even dating.

My focus came around, and I scanned my friends in orderly fashion. They, like me, seemed no worse for the wear.

The roof containing the door we'd apparently fallen through was some twenty feet above us, and whatever opening we'd fallen through had closed itself by providence or a spring-loaded mechanism. Either way, we couldn't be seen from overhead.

I looked around the rest of the large chamber and marveled at the construction. Simple but impenetrable, I surmised.

The wood was weathered but strong as was the rest of the wall structure. Thick, six-by-six beams ran vertically on three sides.

The fourth wall wasn't a wall at all; instead, it was a mammoth gate with two rusted metal rings the size of basketballs on the upper and lower sections, obviously used to open the twelve-foot-high monstrosity.

I immediately thought of *Young Frankenstein* when Gene Wilder expressed his astonishment at the knockers on the Frankenstein Castle door and Teri Garr's character had thanked him.

What knockers indeed.

I glanced at Molek and did a double-take for two reasons. First, his face and general physical appearance were indeed changing. He had more hair on his head, his eyes were even and closer together, his jaw less deformed. His body seemed a bit smaller as well.

The man was continuing his escape from the hell the Master had thought necessary for his development. I didn't know how, but maybe you become what you are surrounded by. We weren't perfect, but the Master was a very bad dream.

The other reason I stared at Molek was because of what he had his hand on. It looked to be this world's version of a circuit breaker. A very old one.

It was much larger and contained a different kind of switch, almost like a beer tap, but it worked.

My frowned returned.

"How did you know where the power switch was?" I asked.

He shrugged. A very human reaction. "I'm not sure. I just saw it in my mind, Seer."

"You just sensed it?"

"Yes."

"Okay, that'll do for now."

But I'm not certain it would. When he spoke, my body tingled, and I saw a brief subdued teal aura surround him. Far different than the dark illumination I'd witnessed when we first met. A good sign, no doubt, but there was something more going on here. I tried to figure it out, but he was blocking me from understanding—consciously or unconsciously, I wasn't sure. Still, I needed to find out what else was going on . . . like the meddlesome old church ladies in North Haven.

Meanwhile, there was another mystery to solve. I turned to Sabrea. I was starting to feel like Sherlock Holmes or Manny Williams.

"You obviously knew where to take us, and I, for one, am grateful. But how did you know this place was here?"

"Navigator, remember? Besides, this is my home, my world. I know of such things."

"Both true. But you didn't know of this one exactly, right?"

For the first time since I'd met this blue Amazon, she hesitated as she mulled over my question and then slowly nodded in my direction.

"You are correct, Seer. I did not know without doubt this sanctuary was present, and I've been alive far too long to believe in luck or providence. So, to answer you, I do not know how we fell into this place."

Fair and honest didn't always mean comfortable. Her response proved that. On top of that, I wasn't even sure why this impromptu save was bothering me so much. Except that it was quite fortunate that I still had my full head of hair.

I still had one more source to grill.

I faced Arzur, who had moved to the door. He'd always been large, but inside this room, he seemed dino-sized. "How about you, big man? Any ideas on how our collective bacons were just saved?"

"I do not, Seer. Perhaps the answer is on the other side of this gate."

Without hesitation, or asking if he should, he pulled it opened, obligatory creepy groan and all.

20-CHAPTER

The next chamber was far different than I would have guessed. And for a seer, I was getting a little tired of guessing and surprises. I'm supposed to be a walking crystal ball, right? Then again, I hardly knew what I was doing and lacked a fair amount of confidence regarding this gift.

Then suddenly I realized that was going to change. This room was the reason why.

In the middle of the second chamber stood a tall triangle, maybe fourteen-feet high. On each leg of this sturdy, steel shape was a leather-covered chair fastened about two feet from the ground, each one a different color and size. In the middle of those three chairs was a three-pronged set of grips or levers that looked for all the world like handles from wooden baseball bats.

Circling the walls about three feet apart going all of the way to the ceiling were soft amber and green lights that looked like the track lights we put in our family room back home—except this lighting was far more riveting and held a mesmerizing, pulsating glow. If I didn't know better, I would have said the lights were alive.

On the far end of the room was a set of ancient, dilapidated steps leading toward the surface, and guarding those steps were two red velvet bands forming the classic "X" shape, which I assumed was to stop anyone from climbing those stairs. Or perhaps warning anyone from entering the room from above.

And last, but certainly not least, in each corner of the room, standing in classic hands-resting-on-sword poses we've all come to know and love, were four stone statues. One effigy for each of us, representing three different races. Arzur's, Sabrea's, and my very own human race.

The fourth representation was a fascinating mixture of all of our peoples.

"Finally," breathed Sabrea.

"Yes, finally," said Arzur.

You know, this whole Triad ritual thing hadn't truly been playing in my thoughts for any significant amount of time. For the most part, I'd simply been trying to stay alive and keep my friends alive since I arrived in Sabrea's land—both times.

As I entered the doorway, this chamber changed that thought process a million times over. This coming together, this joining of three, wasn't a fantasy . . . and my wife says I know a thing or two about fantasy.

This room was the real deal and held echoes of the past, a haunting of unique, committed people, unconditionally drawn and hopelessly compelled to meet together for one magical purpose. I didn't see these beings from the past or in a physical sense, but now their auras spoke to me as well. As did their bonds to each other.

In my life, I'd played sports on a multitude of teams. Each team that went on to become a successful endeavor had one single factor in common: a desire to triumph driven by a strong commitment to one another. My images of the souls who had entered this room to form their own Triads were like that, except on steroids. And not the Major League Baseball kind. The I'm-here-for-you-come-hell-or-high-water kind of strength.

That euphoric sensation made me want to emulate those brave warriors and their sense of brotherhood and sisterhood.

I could feel the excitement—and not just mine because I was as tuned into Arzur and Sabrea as I'd ever been—at the next step in this walk. With each passing second, it was as if the room were coming alive, beckoning us to enter. We did.

We went in together, hand in hand, Arzur's lower left hand and Sabrea's right hand, striding like we owned the place, yet at the same time with an air of reverence.

Molek stayed stationary, contemplating our actions and observing. I knew it without turning around. There was an additional item to address as well. (Isn't there always?) For I realized at that moment, Molek's mission and purpose, at least partially. He was to be our witness to the joining of the Triad. I didn't know for sure if that was in line with this joining ritual, but for us, it was the right call.

"Wait here," I said to Arzur and Sabrea.

At least I think I said it. It truly could have been telepathy, and at this juncture, in this room, I wouldn't have known the difference.

They stopped, and I turned back to Molek. There was no question now that he was smaller, still built like a bodybuilder, but smaller. His eyes were almost even on each side of his smaller nose and held a blue, clear tint that was a bit mysterious and comforting. That sixth sense of seeing kicked in, and I felt another surge of inexplicable kinship for him. His expression told me he'd experienced the same.

I put a hand on his meaty shoulder. "You need to come inside and shut the door. We'll need your vigilance and your protection during this ritual."

"You need me, Seer? Hardly. You will be well during the joining."

His words betrayed his true thoughts, however. His voice had faltered ever so slightly then recovered, but it did little to stop the glistening of tears in his eyes. Our kinship was growing strong.

"We do need you. You're here for a reason. You are our witness. Okay?"

Molek stood taller, steeled his expression, and then grinned. Not the most pleasant sight because his jaw was still a bit sunken and twisted, but far prettier than an hour or two ago.

"I would be honored then to witness a union that has forced the Master into desperate acts to prevent such a joining."

"Follow me."

I heard the door close behind me as I reached Arzur and Sabrea and waited for Molek to stand behind us. We then walked to the tall triangle and without hesitation, climbed into the chairs. We instinctively knew which one we were to sit in. Of course, the size of the chairs made it obvious. I would have felt like Lily Tomlin in that old rocker of hers if I'd gone to Arzur's seat. Sabrea's wasn't much smaller than his.

Slipping into the chair, the cool, smooth wood making that easy, I couldn't help but wonder who had sat here before me. Then I realized no one had. This was my throne, so to speak, made for me specifically. As were the other two for Sabrea and Arzur. The wood was old, grainy, and held the scent of vintage wood and as solid as a rock. It was maybe oak or mahogany but far stronger than any I'd seen.

I would have used newer wood personally, but the age and type of wood was perhaps mandated by tradition or even by necessity. The construction of each chair fit each of us to perfection. How did that happen? Since he knew each of us, was Samuel the builder? Or at least the overseer of the creation of this contraption? Someone else? *Something else?*

Did it matter?

I again thought of what the good guy's version of the Master could be like, and then decided I had more immediate tasks at hand.

Taking one more glance in Molek's direction, I saw a determined guardian standing like Heimdall watching over the Rainbow Bridge leading to Midgard. He could play on my team any day.

I turned back to the others. "Let's get this done. I'm feeling hungry," I said.

"I suspect sustenance will not be a prevalent thought after we begin," said Sabrea.

Smiling, I reached out one hand to her and the other toward Arzur. "We'll see. Never a bad time for a burger."

Sabrea gripped my hand, maybe more like engulfed, with her right and Arzur almost touched my other, and then pulled away.

"What?" I asked.

"I am not positive of which hand to use, Seer."

"The lower."

His look was dubious. "Are you sure?"

"I am. Trust me."

"Does it matter?" asked Sabrea.

"I think it does. But I can't tell you why," I said.

With a nod of his massive head, Arzur clasped his large paw over mine.

The triangle lit instantly with light that rivaled the sun then it continued its evolution transforming into an array of colored auras that instantly morphed into innumerable dots dancing around us. The wall lights joined in.

I'd never seen anything so beautiful in my life. It was as if the universe had been condensed into the scene displayed between and around us. I felt part of all of it as the powerful auras and collective thoughts of countless individuals bombarded my mind.

I was now connected to millions of others but in a far more personal manner, if that made sense. I knew my wife intimately inside and out; but I *existed* with these living dots of light.

I started to speak and couldn't. The sudden appearance of the new vision in my head wouldn't allow it. Instead, it sent me to my knees onto the cool sand, overwhelmed at what this seer gift was showing me. I didn't think I could take it on high volume. I fought to control the overload.

Even the reactive feat of shutting down those colors and thoughts to a less intense level took longer to accomplish than I would have imagined, allowing in just enough of the cornucopia of emotions and eventual fates of many of those beings to drive me to the brink of insanity.

I felt the grip of my friends grow suddenly stronger. We were no doubt sensing and seeing the same things together, and the three of us were bonding—on a different level than slapping someone on the rump after he'd just hit a home run.

We stayed in that state for whatever time was actually time as our lives unfolded to one another. That part was only the beginning for us.

We had no choice but to reveal those closets of secrets as they escaped from the dark and dazzling places in our minds. Yet, there was no discomfort or embarrassment, only truth.

I saw Arzur's past, his endured ridicule for wanting to be something else, and then the acceptance of his fate. This warrior by birth was also a complex, feeling, and dare I say, compassionate creature who understood his calling but longed for the freedom of choice, to explore other possibilities other than killing by his hand. He desired peace, not violence, but would do whatever was necessary.

I saw all of his accomplishments, his training, his joy, what little there had been, and his one place of solitude that was his alone. My heart rejoiced and broke simultaneously.

Sabrea's hand gripped mine even tighter. Her world was spinning, but not from confusion, rather from the sudden knowledge of who she truly was. Her soul was bright with dedication, with purpose, with love, but there was also pain and trepidation. Not for or from the Triad, but from facing her own past.

I saw the source of that fear in an instant and felt the tears form in my closed eyes. She'd lost love, a true love, and there was no worse pain than that for her people. But she held a flicker of hope deep down that she'd love again. That made me smile through the tears.

Through this mind exchange, I had been given an abrupt understanding of just how far this seer, me, could actually see, if I could get a handle on it. I also knew I could help my friends, if they would let me.

That realization led to the next part of this joining, which revealed more than I bargained for and from far too many sources. I wasn't entirely ready for the intense knowledge to come.

My mind seemingly left my body as I sought a way to cope with what I now know had been almost from the beginning of creation and time: conflict. Terrible, eternal conflict.

Fear and hate trying to steal life. Love and peace working to keep it. Each opposing force serving its respective master with no real end in sight, until now. I was horrified at what I saw next.

We, the good guys, were losing. And it was far from pretty. The dark was smothering the light, and doing so quickly.

The knowledge was sobering. An understatement.

I now got it. I understood this fight, this struggle between good and evil wasn't simply a message or some metaphor for moral degradation or cruelty to one another that led to less presents under the Christmas tree.

It was far more. Evil intent was far more than a message or metaphor. Ours was a crusade against what would so maliciously swallow us up and then spit us out into such an indescribably horrendous existence that death would be welcomed. Yet, if I truly saw what I saw, death would not be an option, but a prerogative for the malignant evil that so wanted to rule us all.

As awful as that realization was, more shocking was the rapid decline of those who were willing to stand up for that which was good and right.

Apathy. Terror. Deception. Self-absorption. Each played a part in the equation that led to where these worlds now stood in this battle.

This time I felt the tears trace over my cheeks.

I'd been hopeless a time or two in my life—can anything be more damning than that? But this hopelessness was far darker, far more abysmal. More entrenched. More alive.

In an instant, my thoughts and this repulsive vision were pulled from that dark chasm and brought back to where I sat in this chair. None too soon, I might add. I wasn't sure I could handle any more of what was wrong and not enough of what was right.

Once again, I was dwelling in the midst of Sabrea and Arzur as the dazzling, white lights that had formed by the mingling of our minds began to fade. But before it left completely, it hesitated.

Slowly with a purpose I couldn't define, the light lingered and then seemed to touch, even caress, each of our faces.

Then it was just us. The Navigator. The Warrior. The Seer.

I opened my eyes. I wanted to see the faces of the beings who had formed this Triad and joined together like nothing I'd ever imagined was possible. If I'd ever had children, I supposed this condition was similar, although having kids was probably only up a few notches.

Searching to see their expressions and the accompanying auras, I realized that I'd been wrong. I hate it when that happens.

We four weren't alone.

There was another standing in the middle of the triangle.

21-CHAPTER

The old adage, "Be careful for what you wish for . . ." comes to mind. I suppose the wisdom behind that thought entails one's ability to handle, if you will, the answered prayer or wish.

At this moment, I just might be a prime example of that adage at work. I whined about wanting to see who was on our side, and I was about to get an eyeful.

The being standing in the middle of the framed triangle that hung over the three of us was tall, but not a giant. He was muscular, but not overly so, more like a decathlon athlete. His hair was a golden blond, short and framing his handsome face perfectly.

His clothes were very much like the black material that Sabrea, Arzur, and I wore, except . . . I don't know, brighter? Can black be bright?

His physical appearance aside, there was a presence about him that seduced one's attention. I couldn't take my eyes from him, and I knew, even without looking, that neither Sabrea nor Arzur could resist staring either. There was far more to him than met the eye, of this I was certain.

"Who are you?" I asked.

Pretty brilliant, eh? Not "Where did you come from? How did you get here? How can I make my hair mind like yours?" But the oldest cliché question in the book. I guess I won't be starring in any detective stories soon, but hey, I'm a seer. I see stuff.

"Who do you think I am, Gabriel?"

Fair question. It didn't take an unusually long time to come to me. Swift, I am.

"You're Samuel's boss."

"I prefer the term associate. We are in this battle together. I simply hold a different position and perform in another role. We have the same goals," he said, his smile radiant.

His voice was as calming as any, and I mean any, I've heard. When he spoke, it somehow filtered into the inside of me, creating a serenity that I couldn't stake claim to on the best of days.

After my day to date, calm was nice.

"Do you have a name?"

"I do. You may call me Benjamin."

"I know, not Ben, right?"

He shrugged politely. "Ben, if it makes you feel more comfortable. My name isn't as important as why I am here."

Standing, I brought Arzur and Sabrea out of their chairs with me. We hadn't broken our grips through the joining, and I felt confident with their touch. Or maybe reassured. Was that emotional reserve between us the first sign of the Triad's creation? We'd find out shortly, that I knew.

"You know what I've been thinking, right? You know I've wondered about our side's version of the Master and when he or she was going to jump into this fray and lend a hand."

Such peace in those eyes.

"I do, Gabriel. I do know your thoughts regarding those questions. But I will say that not all things are seen, even by those like me or you."

I exhaled. "Are you it? Are you the one?"

"I'll answer that soon enough. But I have a question for you first. Does it matter that there may be one embodiment that is the antithesis of the evil one you've encountered?"

"Of course—"

I stopped myself and gazed into his eyes again then watched his bright, white aura rise and encircle him. The intensity and beauty of his aura was different than all others thus far, but familiar nonetheless.

It was made of the same living light that had caressed us just after the joining had taken place. There was no question about that. I just didn't know how it mattered or where it fit.

The only way I can truly describe it is, well, pure. Not perfect, but untainted. Unsoiled. Kind. Loyal. Giving. Above all, loving. Not that misguided pretense of love that evolves about what we do for each other, but the kind that shines no matter what we do or don't do.

Those undisputable facts made me want to be better, way better.

I wonder if all that means I'd have to give up chocolate or ice cream and lose a few pounds and stop drinking so much. That was all possible, certainly. But I don't believe it was that kind of life-changing. It had more to do with being better when it came to others and defending what that meant, I think.

The other effect of tapping into that rich aura was seeing his point of view, the one message that he wanted to share with me: that the personification of good isn't encased in one entity, but rather in the combined makeup of the masses. Sort of like the collective good as opposed to the one true source of that goodness.

And I don't mean the Borg. Ben had hair, for crying out loud, and his face wasn't some pale off-blue, and there were no tubes running into his neck.

My thoughts drifted back, and I remembered the time when I went to see my brother Luke, the preacher, at his church building to take him an old brass dish that had been delivered to my house by mistake. It was supposedly from ancient Jerusalem before the time of Christ. He had bought it and wanted to display it at the front of his church's altar. He thought it would be a good reminder of how things had changed in the Christian faith. More directly, that the old Jewish law had been abolished by Jesus' sacrifice on the cross. Something about grace versus works or whatever.

I had rolled my eyes and let him talk. I'd given up fairytales, but trying to be the good brother I always thought I was, I let him finish his story, even though I was thinking of getting away from him as quickly as possible.

He then said Satan had been at play, messing with the arrival of the plate and wanted to screw up his point to the congregation.

I, again, had done what older brothers are supposed to do, this time in a different vein.

I made fun of him and laughed at the thought of a devil or antichrist messing with a small-town church, or with any person, for that matter. That would mean those fairytale bad guys were real. Blah. Blah. Blah.

He'd then proceeded into another one of his friendly lectures, saying that the antichrist the Bible speaks of is not really a person with three sixes stamped on his or her forehead, but instead, a general attitude led by Satan and spread among many, causing more chaos and damage.

I had stared at my brother, trying to remember if he'd been dropped on his head as a kid or if I'd hit him too hard with an errant football. Even a loving brother like myself possessed a crap-odometer, and the needle had just gone to critical.

Sometimes, when you listen to a close relative or friend speak, you think they need to go on medication or experience a serious regimen of electroshock therapy because their take is not the same real-world take the rest of us are living in. Do you know what I mean? That's how I felt at the time.

As I said, it was all I could do to listen politely. I then hugged him and told him to wake up from his dream world and realize this life is it. There ain't any more, that this existence is all she wrote. Religion is only here to make us feel good and take away the fear of dying a physical death, yes?

I told him to pull the underwear out of his crack, then went to the bar with my buddies and made fun of him again, sort of.

As difficult as it had been to swallow that my brother might be a whack job, it was even goofier to think I could have been the one who wasn't right in the head, that any bewilderment regarding the truth was owned wholly by Luke's older brother, Gabriel Andrew Stark. I wonder what he would say about this respite in reality that I've been engaged in over the last few hours?

I mean, come on, who wants to think all of your tires aren't on the road and that you could be wrong?

Not taking my eyes from Ben reinforced the trip down memory lane I'd just taken. I don't know about Satan or Jesus, per se, but Ben's point was well suffered.

Good and evil, whatever or whomever that entailed exactly, weren't going to be sending each other party invites any time soon and, to put it even more succinctly, there was a growing sense of just how universal the effect could be if the good guys gave up the good fight.

I shifted my feet slightly as I remembered all those grandiose movies where the good guys are outnumbered, out-weaponed, out-dinosaured, out-whatevered, and the hero or heroine proclaims that they must fight to the end. Lots of those folks died in the land of make-believe, and it wasn't always the end of the evil either.

Damn sequels. I hate that little puppet with the red hair and scar.

The enchanting idea of that was fine while sitting in a movie theater eating popcorn and holding Kara's hand. Here, in this spot, in this reality, it didn't seem so noble. Or at least the prospect of going down with the ship was served with a side of fear of the unknown at the end of this life. Although who would have thought what I was now a part of was "reality"?

Looking toward him again, I did the famous double-take. Ben was no longer there.

Not a sign of him, his aura, or even an ancient, decrepit book on how to kick evil's collective ass. Talk about a bestseller, by the way.

No timeless scroll to unravel. No quirky, insignificant-to-the-naked-eye artifact to channel the aggregate power of good and burn the heart out of evil on Sabrea's earth. Not even a Hershey's bar with almonds as a reward, which sounds incredibly good at the moment.

Ben was just gone. His perception of what I, or we, needed was far different than my own. Did he really think that was all I required to take the next step in this journey? A little knowledge? A history lesson, in essence? He didn't even tell me where the fake leg came from.

I wanted to be angry, but that wasn't an option I realized after a few seconds reflecting on what we had just experienced and dwelling on Ben's words.

The truth was that he'd answered my concern with a question, but that simple question-answer had been far more than that. I at least got that much.

He was telling me that we weren't alone, but we needed to find the help required to fight the good fight. It was there. I just had to use what I had to see it. Shouldn't be a problem. Hey, after all, I'd been a seer for, like what, twelve days? I was practically a veteran. If I could have rolled my eyes, I would have.

Now I know why Frodo and Sam wanted to go home to the Shire. I suddenly wanted a Shire of my own. I had a brief but vivid picture of Kara in one of those dresses the female hobbits wore at party time. She was pretty hot, except for the big feet thing.

I sighed. No doubt Ben and Samuel were on the same team; team cryptic. At least I could call him Ben.

"It seems, Seer, that you've received an answer to what you've been pondering," said Sabrea, her blue hands still firmly entrenched in Arzur's and mine.

"It was an answer, no doubt about that," I said.

"Was it what you required, Seer?" asked Arzur.

"Good question. We'll find out soon."

I stood looking at my friends, shot another look toward Molek, who hadn't moved from his position, as stoic as ever, and realized another truth.

Yes, I know, realizing truths seemed to be the rule of the day.

We had one more step to make to solidify, to finish off this Triad-joining thing.

Sabrea and Arzur knew it as well; their miens said so.

"Are we all ready?" I asked.

"We, as your people say, were born ready, Gabriel," said Sabrea, another dazzling smile accompanying her words.

Arzur nodded.

I closed my eyes and began a process I'd never performed but understood as well as I knew the color of my own eyes.

Blue, right?

I pictured their auras, and they came into full view instantaneously. Sabrea's as bright as any shade of orange had a right to be, Arzur's yellow aura taking on growing luster with every passing second.

The third aura, a wide light that flashed through three colors, blue, green, and purple, was no doubt mine. I hadn't experienced my own aura as of yet and was fascinated by the concept that I had one. I suppose it was a little like hearing your voice on a recording device for the very first time. The operative question was always "is that me?" Unless one was performing karaoke while pounding down a few. Then the response is more like: "I should have been a star, man."

The three auras slowly pulsed and swirled like jellyfish in the ocean, and then began to move closer together, reaching toward one another and almost touching, but not quite. The tantalizing dance was intoxicating on every level. I knew what was about to happen.

I watched and waited for my friends to catch up. When finally, and in a true sense, I knew that Arzur and Sabrea were seeing exactly what I was and in real time, I concentrated and pushed however seers push. The three auras hesitated, shimmered, grew bright, and then melted together in a blink.

The effect was brilliant as the joining of those lights became exactly that.

There was no more rapid upload of deep, dark secrets and unconfessed sins shared between us. No mental anguish at being who we are, or who we are not, no glimpse into what makes us happy or angry, just a total infusion of three lives who now were one in almost every concept except physical. We still had our own bodies; at least I was sure of that much.

That being said, I knew that I would be able to hear their very heartbeats from worlds away, or hear the rumble of thunder through their ears, if wanted and when I wanted. As long as I trusted my gift.

That wasn't all. I also knew without a doubt I would know the second they might be in danger or were hurt or worse, just as directly as if I were standing in their shoes. Or in Arzur's case, his feet.

This marriage of souls, if you will, was the most intense and yet freeing experience of my life.

Well duh!

All this if for no other reason than to confirm there was something that bound us all, every living thing together and there was a life force beyond what the senses could show us.

I know. No surprise there, right? But to have faith in something, then to glean the actual knowledge that the faith or hope, or whatever term you want to use, is a bonafide done deal, is like going from the little leagues to the majors.

The next moment, we were on our knees, still tightly gripping each other's hands.

Our auras had separated again but were still so dazzling that they forced me to tone them down so I could see what was coming next.

They lingered close together for a few moments longer, then slowly separated taking on the appearance of an interlinked, three-sphere version of the international Olympic rings.

They no longer held a color of their own—the three identical sea-green auras reflected our joining as a Triad, each completed and secure individually, yet as one. I watched the glows settle first around Arzur, then Sabrea, then me. Then visual silence.

I'd always been pretty much a relaxed guy during my adult life, but the peace and calm I felt at this moment were beyond what any TV commercial could possibly sell. Well, at least any that didn't have Vanna performing the pitch.

Basking in peace is never a bad thing so I did just that for a while longer, then almost reluctantly, I stood with my two friends, who were now far more than friends, and we released our grips on each other. For one brief moment, I thought I would panic at the absence of their touch, but the idea dissipated, replaced by more surprises, even to a seer.

Arzur stepped close, bent his head toward mine, and rested it on my forehead—part of it anyway because his dome was truly a dome—and then whispered to me.

"I will die for you, Seer, if needed. You are my brother like none other."

He stepped back, picked me from the ground, and kissed my cheeks, then winked. In a manly way, of course.

Would wonders never cease? Arzur with humor?

I laughed out loud, but couldn't truly speak in response. This giant had touched me with his actions. Actions, that oddly enough, were spur of the moment for him and something I hadn't seen coming, but knew was there inside him.

He then repeated the encounter with Sabrea, and I saw the tears glisten in her eyes as she only nodded her response. God of wonders, the woman had no words, at least for a moment. Until she strode to me, that is.

"I saw much, Seer. Yet not as much as you, I know. But I, like Arzur, will walk, fight, and serve beside you both, until there is no reason to or until death includes me in its mysterious journey."

My turn to not speak.

The vision of my wedding day rumbled across my memory, and I recalled in 3-D detail just how much emotion cascaded through my soul when Kara had said "I do" to my brother Luke's question on whether she would take me as her husband.

There is nothing like someone accepting you, loving you, unconditionally, their heart wide open, imperfections and all. It adds a value to each of us that can't possibly be measured in any way I'd experienced until now. Double it, if you will.

I nodded, cleared my throat, and felt the smile grow across my face.

At least we had that going for us.

The next moment, my mind ricocheted in a different direction. A less than pleasant one, I might add.

The gate we'd dropped through to get into these subterranean chambers was now the focus of our recent pursuers. I could see it.

And they weren't happy.

22-CHAPTER

Assessing the situation like I knew what I was doing, I barked out orders. Pretty impressive, if you ask me.

"Molek. Secure those doors to this chamber. The Culroids will be knocking on the other door to the surface, and I'm in no mood to let them in to this one, yes?"

"I agree. Let me see what I can do," he said as he hurried to the other room.

"Sabrea. As navigator, figure out the safest direction for us to travel, and let's do it."

"Aye, aye, Seer."

But I knew she was already on it as she headed toward the dark corners of the chamber.

I turned to my four-armed warrior and knew he'd already had an inkling of what I was going to ask.

I asked it any way.

"Arzur, I want you to destroy this Triad chair, okay?"

He tilted his massive head and stared at me. Not the questioning glance that goes with you-are-an-idiot that you sometimes receive from people who work for you, or even from children, when you tell them to follow instructions. Instead, it was the look that says "I need an explanation."

Luckily, I had one, even though I wasn't quite sure where the knowledge came from.

I stepped toward him and stopped two feet away. "We can't leave this intact. Somehow, if it stays in one piece, they'll be able to get a read on what happened here and who it happened to. I don't understand what might be termed as magic or psychic energy or just flat-out deduction, but I know it will be trouble if this isn't destroyed. No one else can use this joining triangle. If someone tries, it could work against us. It was ours and has to stay that way."

By now, the din above was crescendoing into a dull roar.

I don't know how many—wait. I do. The eyes inside my head, if you will, were as crystal clear as if I'd been atop a high sand dune watching the scene unfold in full HD exposure. Even the collective black auras couldn't mask what I saw.

There were four thousand eight hundred seventy-six Culroids marching almost on top of us. One hundred thirty-three flying creatures—called Argats, by the way—swooping around in an organized version of chaos. I received a sudden close-up of one of them and felt myself flinch.

Their faces were not unpleasant to look at, almost fairylike. Wide-eyed and delicate, giving them a certain beauty. We all need a positive attribute, right? That, however, was where the splendor ended.

Their bodies and double wings were dull gray and scaly, like dragonflies, that ran right up to their chins. Each possessed forked tails with poisonous venom that would render virtually anything paralyzed and eventually dead. That was strange and unnerving enough, but their two-inch teeth were uniformly sharpened. Good for ripping flesh from bones.

I felt myself swallow hard. This was no Disney flick, and these creatures had a far different agenda than entertainment.

Trailing behind the Culroids were twelve wide-backed burden animals, each the size of small houses, resembling six-legged rhinos only with bulging eyes and two tails.

I saw them all so vividly that I could almost taste the dour cud the animals were working in their mouths and smell their zoo-like scent.

I don't think Christian Dior would be putting that singular odor in a bottle and marketing it any time soon. Although, I've smelled some classic perfumes that may have originated from a relative of these rhino-legged creatures.

Arzur touched me, and I jumped.

"Did you hear me, Seer?"

I had not.

"No. I was checking out our visitors, all forty-eight hundred of them. What did you say?"

"I asked you if you were sure that you wanted this chair destroyed. It represents much. And that isn't so many as I thought." His semi-grin looked out of place.

"It does. Like I said, it can't get into anyone else's hands, period. Turn it into firewood. And that many beings who want to see how our insides look on the outside doesn't bother you?"

He did it again, that half-cocked grin, then said, "Move toward the large doors."

Five ear splitting hacks with those battle swords he carried, and mission accomplished. He was powerful, but it had been almost too easy. He confirmed that.

"There may be magic afoot here indeed, Seer. The destruction of that ancient wood should have taken time, even for a warrior such as myself."

"Hey. We'll take all of the help we can get."

I knew that was an understatement, but since we'd met Ben, I held a premonition that we might see more of this unexpected help. We could use it.

Sabrea joined us, as did Molek, and it was time to get to it.

Sorry. I don't have a better word than "it." What was going on, and what we had to do next, wasn't explainable in a few words or moments of time, maybe not even in a lifetime. "It" was just next on the menu.

"Molek?"

"The doors are fortified. I secured the entrance that allowed us to fall into the other chamber. It has a steel bolt that will not allow the door to unhinge unless it is broken. It won't last forever, but will suffice," he said, his voice far smoother than any time before.

His face was now almost fully transformed from the grotesque creature who'd wanted to castrate me and put my head on a pole to, dare I say it, human form. Not a bad-looking man, either, in a scarred, rugged, bad-boy way. His auburn hairline had crawled down into a semi-widow's peak and flowed down his neck. He had a small scar over his nose and a thin line running from his left eye to the right side of his chin that hadn't been there before. Throw in the rope burn or three around his neck, and his look was complete.

If we got out of this alive, I wanted to talk with him because, oddly enough, I couldn't sense much more about his past than he'd revealed to me.

I turned to our navigator.

"Sabrea?"

"There are three pathways we can take. We can go out the way we came in, kill all of the ugly bastards, even the winged wenches, and then after, locate a house of refreshment, which I'm greatly familiar with, and celebrate our victory with intoxicating drink and too much food and maybe you can see my breasts."

She laughed.

I shook my head.

"Ahh, okay. What about option two?" I asked.

"We could attempt to scale the old stairway blocked with the red crosses that will lead to the surface and put us in the same situation as our first option, only farther away from the horde for a moment or two."

"What is the third option, not truly caring for either of the first."

"It won't be pleasant either, Gabriel," she said.

I couldn't see exactly what she was talking about, but her sense of trepidation was real. What the hell is wrong with me? I just went through this joining, and now I couldn't tell what she had on her mind? I dismissed it as nerves or something akin to that.

"I'm betting it beats the hell out of certain death, after we've been tortured and denutted or deboobed, for, oh I don't know a week or so. So let's have it."

She raised her eyebrows and tilted her head. "Deboobed? That does not sound pleasant. I will tell you. There is a small opening with a sealed door in the very darkest shadow of this chamber. It is marked with the language of the old ones. It equates to what you would call an emergency exit."

"This qualifies as an emergency, I'd say."

"Beneath that opening lies a narrow passageway, no more than a tunnel, that hasn't been used for centuries."

"Where does that passageway lead?" asked Arzur.

"It follows a winding path that will eventually lead to an opening in the opposite direction this scourge came from. It could take about two miles of travel, crawling at times, in your earth's terms."

"That seems reasonable to avoid this army, for now," I said, knowing there was a big-ass "but" coming. There always is.

She looked at Arzur, then to me, then to Molek. There was no sparkle in those fuchsia eyes this time.

"What? Is the passageway large enough for all of us? Is it filled with water? Are there reruns of *I Love Lucy* playing on large-screen TVs the whole trip?"

Her bright smile came and then disappeared in the same moment.

"None of those fears are true. Even though I'm not entirely sure what a TV is, I understand your thoughts. Now I need you to see for yourself."

"Okay, that's what I do. Let me see if I can get a picture of what we might run into."

But I couldn't. I closed my eyes and tried again. Nothing came to me. Only darkness and an amplified dose of Sabrea's original anxiety. Was it me? Was there something going on where I couldn't use my gift?

Samuel had said, as did Ben, that not all things would be available to me. Most, but not all. That people and other things could block the visions and sights. But not the sense of who and what the essence of someone or something was. I didn't like how this tunnel felt either.

"I can't get a read, but we have no other viable choice. Take us to it."

She turned and began to trot toward the back of the huge room.

As I moved to follow, I heard it. Not just the noise but the intent.

The dedicated clamor above us had increased. There was now a purposeful, rhythmic pounding echo throughout the lower chambers as the dark legion began work on the trapdoor that brought us to this place.

I picked up the pace and, a few moments later, stood in front of the sealed entrance beside my fellow travelers.

The symbols of the ancient ones, as Sabrea had called them, weren't exactly all that ancient because I could read good, old-fashioned English with the best of 'em.

It wasn't an emergency exit, per se, according to the stark warning on the door.

"ENTER AT RISK OF CERTAIN DEATH" wasn't exactly a Get Out of Jail Free card, now was it?

Arzur nudged me. "I see you are not happy with the language on the door, yes?"

"No, I'm not. I'm starting to consider Sabrea's first option."

"Ha! I knew there was a warrior in there somewhere," she said.

"What say you, Seer?" asked Molek.

Shrugging, I stepped back and motioned for him to have at it.

As he raised his sword, the thick wooden door suddenly rasped open from right to left. We were instantaneously greeted with the rush of age-old air riddled with several undefinable stale odors that I didn't readily recognize and a decay that could have only come from one source.

I'd not been around dead bodies all that often, although that joyous experience was increasing by the hour, but I knew death when I smelled it.

"It would seem we've been issued an invite," said Molek.

"It would," I said.

I had no vision of what was inside this seemingly unpleasant destination, and the human in me was certain that annihilation, the painfully slow kind, awaited us courtesy of the beings on the surface who were now closing in on us. Sort of like dogs but way more determined.

Glancing at my posse one more time, I raised my hands in surrender.

"Come into my abode said the spider to the fly."

I stepped through the entrance . . .

23-CHAPTER

. . . And was promptly pulled off the uneven ground by the nape of my neck and placed behind Sabrea and Arzur and in front of Molek.

The female was strong, I get that, but to lift an almost two-hundred-pound man from the floor with a flick of her wrist revealed more strength than I'd suspected. So much for "seeing" that particular aspect of my beautiful navigator.

And yes, my man-pride was temporarily injured.

"Just where do you think you are going?" she asked, her arms folded.

"Down this path. In the event you need to be reminded, we have to get the hell out of Dodge."

"I do not need to be reminded, Gabriel. I am the navigator, and I lead the way. You have tried to see who or what awaits us down this path and cannot. I can at least choose the correct and shortest direction to a safer destination."

She was right; I did need to be reminded.

I bowed, my arm extended. "Lead the way, fair maiden."

Sabrea bent to me and kissed me again, this time on the lips. "You are such a gentleman. I pray we live long enough to get naked, as your people say, Gabriel Stark."

"What? I'm married, remember?"

She threw her head back and laughed. "Focus, Seer. I jest with you."

"Yeah, yeah. Let's go."

I'd be a liar if said I didn't wonder what a blue woman looked like without her clothes though. Come on, who wouldn't?

We entered the passageway a second time, Sabrea, Arzur, me, and Molek bringing up the rear.

The path was black, hardened dirt with a subtle odor that reminded me of garden dirt back home, but the tunnel had been cut through pure rock that resembled granite. The ceiling was around eight-feet high, so Arzur was standing up straight as we walked, but I suspected that would change. Actually, I knew it would.

After we moved about twenty feet into the tunnel, the door behind us, predictably, like something from a Vincent Price movie, closed with a dull thud. None of us glanced back. It had been a given. Whoever, or whatever, had opened it sure as sin wasn't going to leave it that way.

When the door closed, we lost all light, and I suddenly felt like I was in one of those scary maze houses my friends and I would go through at the county fair. That thought brought on a fast desire to be back in one of them again. At least I knew how those sojourns ended.

The pitch black was quickly interrupted by two sources of light. No, make that three. Molek was holding a small, metallic cylinder that he'd apparently retrieved from his belt. The globe was six inches long and four inches around, radiating a hard, white light that made the area behind us seem like noon on a bright summer day.

Sabrea was holding a slightly smaller version of Molek's light, but the effect was the same as it lit the path ahead.

The third source of illumination was a little more complicated.

The very walls began to emanate a subtle yellowish-green glow running in patterned veins reminiscent of deposits of gold in an underground mine. The combination of the two light globes and the winding pattern made the walls pulse like they were in motion.

"What metal is this?" I asked.

"It's not metal," said Sabrea.

"Sure it is."

"It is not, Seer."

"What then?"

"They are countless biologics. They absorb light and then in turn amplify that light. They are called bender worms. Soon, we will not need these globes."

I suspected the worms operated in the same manner of bioluminescent creatures, like fireflies or ocean plankton.

I reached to touch the wall, and Molek quickly grabbed my arm.

"They are also very poisonous if they happen to break your skin with their tiny teeth. They are often used to torture those who oppose the Master."

Jerking my hand back, I looked at him.

"Just how does that work?"

He shrugged. "The bodies of the infected swell, their eyes bulge to three times their normal size, and fingers look the size of small logs. Then, in a very synchronized fashion, their body parts began to explode, usually the gonads first, then the eyes, then the rest."

I stopped long enough to cross my legs.

"Let us continue," said Arzur. "And mind your gonads, Seer."

Was that another smile from Arzur?

"You too, Warrior."

"I do not have them."

Another fact I'd missed during the joining, although that hadn't been much about the physical. Still, no gonads?

"What? What do you have? Never mind. I don't care to know."

"You should see more and listen less," said Arzur.

"Okay, smartass. Seeing your sexual organs, or lack thereof, isn't at the top of my list of things to do."

"Just follow me. You can compare gonads later," said Sabrea.

We followed her without exposing ourselves, but I wanted to.

After we'd continued another two hundred yards or so, we no longer needed the lights but that didn't make the start of our trip any easier. The trail was winding and headed slightly downward. I wasn't in love with the fact that we were going deeper into Sabrea's earth, and even less enthralled with the fact we were underground and our sight was somewhat limited because of the twists and turns in the path. But that's why Sabrea was with us. She stepped with confidence, and that was worth something, especially since I still couldn't get my seer crap together.

I had no idea what was going on with any emotion or aura regarding any living creature but me and an occasional tidbit of insight I could gather from Arzur and Sabrea.

The question remained, why?

Why would this location or set of circumstances inhibit my sight, so to speak? And why was Sabrea able to navigate? Arzur could always be a warrior, but part of his gift was to know when and how to battle, so maybe neither of us really needed our gifts here. That was my best guess, and it would have to do for now. I'd have to accept it and move on.

The song "Let it Go" came to mind. (I never could hit those high notes.)

Besides, we had an army to get away from. I found myself hoping this was the proper method to accomplish just that.

We continued down the trail in silence. Something a bit unusual for this group, but I didn't need the gift to sense our discomfort in working our way down a path that hadn't apparently been traveled in a century or two.

I did my best to focus my observational skills on this path in front of me, rather than dwell on where we were headed. That was Sabrea's gig.

It seemed rather benign and not worthy of the warning that had been sinisterly placed on the door. Nevertheless, I took it upon myself to constantly scrutinize the ceiling as we traveled because in all of those horror movies I'd seen, the beast, the killer, the monster, or whatever hanging around on the ceiling and the hapless idiots it was stalking never thought about looking up until it was too late.

I'm far too smart to be suckered in by that clichéd situation, seer or not.

I also took time to notice the floor and walls for odd markings and tracks that couldn't possibly be human or related to Sabrea's people. The only thing I noticed was some old scratchy indentations that occasionally interrupted the bender worm. They didn't appear to be anything alarming, but how in the hell did I know for sure? Not being able to use my seer skill was frustrating after it had been at my disposal and then taken away.

After we'd traveled another uneventful twenty minutes or so, I was beginning to believe this was going to be easier than anticipated. Good. God knew we could use a break here. Escaping that army of evil Culroids, flying Argats, and other assorted piss heads was important, but what to do about them after our getaway was another matter entirely. Then Sabrea, after turning a particularly sharp corner, abruptly stopped, staring at the ground a yard in front of her feet.

The end of the smooth trip through this catacomb was upon us.

I stepped past Arzur.

"Why have we stopped?"

"Do you not see?" Arzur asked.

"Not with my inside eyes. They seem to be blocked and—"

In the last two days, I was becoming accustomed to halting my speech in midsentence. It was a knack I developed after seeing some of the junk I'd seen lately. I was now perfecting that syndrome.

This reason for my lost words was up there with the best of the best.

On the dark dirt in front of Sabrea lay a large pile of stacked bones, the accompanying shadows adding to the starkness of the configuration.

The bleached bones were of different sizes and different orientations, yet they were amassed in an orderly fashion, slightly faded bones crossing other less faded bones, large on the bottom, smaller bones situated on the top. There was only the slightest hint of biomaterial near the ends of some of the smaller bones. They'd appeared to have been efficiently cleaned. The small grooved teeth marks on each of the bones told me how that cleaning had been accomplished.

"Crap," I whispered.

On each of the four corners of the display rested a skull. The two smaller skulls on the front of the display—human-sized, I guessed—each had remnants of the respective victim's hair, and one was red or blond, the other black. The two larger ones, one much larger than the others, had been stripped of any strands of hair that I could see.

There didn't seem to be any external injuries to the skulls, like a head bashing incident had taken place, but as if to make up for such a macabre possibility, I watched dozens of tiny red beetle-like creatures dancing in the skulls' eye sockets.

"What is this?" asked Sabrea.

"I've not seen such a shrine either," said Arzur, gripping the hilt of his sword.

Molek moved to a step behind Arzur, brushing my arm as he did and forcing me off balance so that I had to touch the dirt leading to the stack of bones, brushing one skull as I regained my equilibrium.

My fingers burned as my mind came alive. I then heard Molek speak in a faraway sort of manner as I was, in the blink of an eye, transported somewhere else.

Seeing. It's the gift that keeps on giving . . . when it damn well wants to.

Oddly enough, I stood on the same path we'd been walking on but not in the same location, not by a longshot. The bender-worm glow shimmering from the walls was dimmer, more subdued, and the tunnel itself had grown even more narrow and short.

I doubted that Arzur could stand normally or get his shoulders through the opening unless he was some sort of contortionist. He wasn't. I knew that much.

The air moved faster, almost a breeze, and the bouquet riding that wind had taken on different properties as well. It was now more of a pleasant stench. Repulsive but sweet. Something like ancient scents and new odors at the same time. Kind of like sweet and sour chicken.

I know what you're thinking, but it is true nonetheless, and right now, a heaping plate of that from Ying's place in downtown North Haven sounded better than making love. I'm serious.

I glanced in the direction I suspected we'd been coming from and saw only another sharp jut of jagged rock as it cut into the path, suggesting another severe twist. I looked in the other direction and saw a more gentle turn in the trail, although it appeared even more diminished.

That wasn't all.

I heard water running, like a small waterfall cascading into a pool or stream. Peculiarly enough, I was struck with how thirsty I was too.

I also think I have to pee.

Yep. I feel like I'm at the office.

Resisting the urge to relieve myself on the spot, I stepped down the narrowing path toward the sounds of traveling H2O.

Moving sixty feet or so, the sound grew louder, more inviting. I heard some other ambient sounds but they didn't really register because I was entirely engrossed with the possibility and concept of moving water. Hypnotized even.

I was now hurrying, ignoring everything except the draw of the water.

What the hell's wrong with me? I need to be more cautious, but what does it matter? There is no real danger here. What's so scary about water?

Then, most unexpectedly, I broke into a wide, spacious hollow that resembled the second chamber where my Triad had formed.

Do you know what it's like when you walk into a room or turn on a video and the first unpleasant thing you see shocks you because it's so far out of any normal expectation that you have to reorient yourself?

That's me, one hundred fold. And there sure as hell wasn't anything pleasant about the creatures I locked eyes with.

Four human-sized beasts, fangs over upper and lower lips, turned away from what they were doing to size me up.

I wonder if they have to decide which of their three eyes running the width of their foreheads to focus with first, or if it just comes naturally.

The black, hair-covered beings were dressed in nothing except tattered loincloths that dangled around muscular thighs. Their arms were large and strong, as evidenced by what they were doing. Their chests, supporting three nipples, were identical to one another's in shape and tension. Any linebacker in football would have been proud to have a chest like these four possessed.

The attending silence as these four stood frozen, eyebrows raised (I think), was stark, but perhaps not as pointed as their gory activity.

There wasn't any waterfall. There wasn't any gentle underground stream. The echoing splash of running liquid currently originated from the two Culroids, held high in the air, as the gushing blood drained from their jaggedly sliced throats. The blood-drained pile of bodies behind the four creatures told me that these Culroids weren't the first to contribute to the crimson stream that ran into the lengthy metal trough, which ended in the large amber cistern some ten feet away from me.

There was motion to my right, and I swung in that direction. These four holding the Culroids weren't alone. Hardly.

There must of have been another forty creatures, all having the same basic appearance except for the color of their hair. Some were more auburn than black, and there was some variance in height. Other than that, long fangs and triple eyes were the order of the moment.

Oddly enough, I heard no vocalizations, as one might expect from a seemingly mindless horde of blood drainers. You know, like grunts and growls and disparaging remarks about the Green Bay Packers or the Dallas Cowboys.

Let it not be said that I was slow this time. I turned to sprint back to where I'd come from . . . and, like a bad dream, could not. I actually couldn't see my feet, even though I was certain I was pumping my legs as hard as I could.

I then glanced over my shoulder to see just how close I was to becoming part of the blood mix and found that none of these creatures were moving either. In fact, other than what I perceived as surprised glances when I'd first entered this chamber, not one of these nightmares actually were paying any real attention to me.

After a brief period of puzzlement, I knew why. I wasn't really at this location at all.

Another side-light to this seer gig.

By touching the dust around the stack of bones and the skulls, I had opened a door to a different place in time, maybe only an hour or two, but definitely into the future . . . and what awaited us down the path we believed would get us away from the army that would see us dead. Those bones unquestionably belonged to my party of four.

I shivered.

Talk about double-jeopardy or even quad-jeopardy.

Knowing what was behind us and knowing what was before us gave us choices; the lesser of two sure horrifying deaths was the prize.

I also had a sense this choice wasn't just about the number of enemies on either front. I suspected that given an opportunity, Arzur could kill hundreds of Culroids and the flying Argats before sheer numbers overwhelmed him, maybe half as much for Molek and Sabrea and I. We'd put a dent in that army, but we'd lose.

The blood spillers in this cavern numbered less than fifty, as far as I could see, a light workout for Arzur. I could just hold his bag and pick my teeth until he finished. Yet, there was something more dangerous and sinister about this setup than met the eye, and even with the building strength of my gift, I couldn't put a finger on exactly what that might be. (The whole less-than-powerful seeing thing was bothering me. We'd joined, the three of us, and I'd *felt* the power escalate exponentially then. I know, I know. I said it before, but it was becoming even more frustrating. I felt I needed my gift more than ever, but it was being denied me at times. This forced me to use what my mama gave me, whatever the hell that meant in the here and now.)

Traps? Venom? Sheer strength? Distracting Sirens? Reruns of *90210*? I'm totally clueless.

I inhaled and released the air in my lungs because a deep breath always allowed me to slow down a bit. There was that sweet and pungent scent again. Did I say that sweet-and-sour anything sounded really good right now? Well, except Culroid, but if it was a delicacy in Sabrea's world, I was willing to give it a shot.

I blinked and smacked my forehead.

For the second time in a minute, I had another revelation. And, by cracky, this one hadn't really required any supernatural gift, just simple deduction.

That pleasant odor would have us all unconscious and laying in the dirt before we reached this part of the trail. That was how this predator/prey situation worked for them. No fuss, no muss, just unconscious donors to their grotesque blood bank. It was pretty ingenious and undoubtedly effective, if the intended prey had no idea what was happening.

The thing is, *I* did know what's happening.

That situation would no doubt explain the lack of damage on our future skeletons and why those bones could be stacked so neatly.

Taking another deep breath, I closed my eyes and willed myself back to my friends, I hoped. The next time I opened my peepers, I could be looking at the Emerald City of Oz or inside the Whitehouse's Oval Office (scary, right?), for all I know. I am, however, armed with information that would save our lives, and millions more perhaps, if I read this situation right.

Then again, I've always been sort of optimistic, and reading things correctly is still new to me.

24-CHAPTER

Well, wonder of wonders.

I opened my eyes and was immediately staring at the collective concerned faces of my traveling companions.

"Hey. I made it back." I said, sitting on the cool sand, staring up at them.

"And just where is it that you ventured?" asked Arzur. "All we witnessed was your frail vessel fainting like, what do you say, a frightened school girl."

"He speaks the truth, Gabriel. It has been long since I witnessed the whites of a man's eyes roll up in their head like that. It had a certain unsettling quality," chimed in Sabrea.

Even Molek spoke before I could answer. "We thought you had been overcome by one of the Master's demons or spells. I have seen such a thing."

"One at a time. And I'm not frail or a frightened school girl or demon-possessed. I'm quite manly, in the event you all haven't noticed, and my mind is as clear as it's ever been. So help me up and we'll talk."

"If you say so, Manly Seer," said Sabrea, giggling.

I know I've said it before, but I love this woman.

She had to be a Viking in another life because everything that entailed serious situations or referred to imminent danger and possible death was funny to her. If truth be known, my instincts alerted me to something along that line and I was sure she at least had a kindred spirit related to those conquerors. Weirdly enough, my Seer insight was returning, and I *knew* that of her. I know what Ben had said as we came out of the joining, that I wouldn't see everything, and it was now making more sense. Maybe someone like me could only handle so much aura-spotting and insight at a time.

A flash later, I was standing on surprising solid legs, thanks to one fleeting yank of my arm from Arzur's two right limbs.

Did I mention that this creature's strength would make Hercules look like a toddler?

"Apparently when I touched the dirt or maybe the bones, it sent me into a different place in time, the future, I think, but not too far, maybe a few hours."

"How do you know that?" asked Sabrea.

"It had to be. These bones are ours, not more than a few hours from now."

I pointed to the stack and promptly watched them disappear in a ripple of light and veiled transparency.

For one of the few times since I'd met these beings, they, and I, were momentarily speechless.

Arzur spoke first. "What has just happened?'

I had the answer.

"Listen, and I don't want to confuse anyone, but that vanishing act was to be expected. That future isn't about us any longer."

"How do you know that, Seer?" asked Arzur.

"A fair question. By touching the bones, I was able to see a distance up the trail and see what would have been in store for us if we had continued down the path. I'm able, at least in this instance, to see some time into the future so the seer in me is functioning on some level. That group of three-eyed beasts—you should have seen them!—would have drained our blood and then skinned what was left of us, leaving the bones in memoriam."

"Do you really mean those bones were ours?" asked Molek.

I thought about what Molek said. Were they truly our bones? Or merely a representation of what was a possible future, and they were not truly substantial? I decided that there were some things one cannot explain and we had little time for a session at the round table.

I studied his face, which had now fully reverted to his human form.

"I think that's a great question. Real or a manifestation of the future, those bones served their purpose, and we're alive, at least for a while as long as we don't go farther into this tunnel."

Sabrea stepped closer to me, her incredible eyes looking me over as if searching for something she'd lost.

"What?"

"What you are suggesting is that we turn around and go back to face a certain death. Surely we can overcome whatever lies ahead now that you know what is there."

I motion for Arzur and Molek to come as close as the blue Amazon.

"I want you all to put a hand on my shoulder. Arzur, just one."

"Is that humor, Seer?"

"No, self-preservation. Your hands are heavy. Just do it. I think I can show you what is there and why it won't work to continue ahead."

Each of them put a strong hand on one of my shoulders. Molek was the last and almost reluctant to do it, but he did, after what seemed to be a serious, but quick internal discussion.

I released my suppression of their auras, which also released my gift, and concentrated on what I'd seen.

It was over in thirty seconds. They saw all that I had. I felt the revulsion excreting from each of them.

I shuddered at their impressions.

After hasty removals of big paws from my shoulders, my comrades carried a different look of surprise and accompanying dread, but the connotation from what I showed them was the same for each: that road ahead was best untraveled.

"Drainers," whispered Sabrea. "I thought them part of old wives' tales."

"Clearly, they are not. But there weren't many of them. We would only have to get past the sinister fragrance, and we could continue down the path," said Arzur.

"But that would seem to be impossible given what the Seer has just showed us," said Sabrea.

"And let's not forget that no matter what we think we can scheme up to run the Drainer gauntlet, so to speak, the vision of the bones warns me that we won't make it past them," I said.

I wish I could handle silence.

Maybe it was because of my old job. The call center was always in motion, and there was never a second when the office was at peace. That or the fact that silence was predicated on a reflective state of mind that was seldom experienced in my life. Or the fact that each of us was contemplating which death was better: death by Drainer versus death by the Master's legion of shitheads.

Sabrea picked me up from the ground (something I was becoming used to), and those unbelievable fuchsia eyes bore into mine.

"You are the Seer, Gabriel. And a special one, because I have never heard of one that is able to do what we have witnessed from you. I will lead us to wherever you determine. Arzur will be the warrior that he is called to be as a part of this Triad. Molek will follow as well. You must decide."

Great.

Twelve days ago, I was singing *The Christmas Song* with Nat King Cole in my car and looking forward to Christmas morning with my wife and dog. And I had both legs.

Since then, I'd been in a horrific car crash, met Samuel the white-suited whatever the heck he was, seen auras around folks, met someone who said she was my real mother, killed a four-armed giant, become part of a bizarre Triad on a parallel earth, met some Master dudette who tried to play me—and looked like my wife to boot—just to name a few things that would qualify me for the local nuthouse. Never mind Culroids, Argats, and Drainers.

Now I'm supposed to decide which way we should die?

I need a Reese's Peanut Butter Cup, Santa. A big one.

The thought of where to go next was clear, I suppose, but to say it out loud was hardly good for keeping morale high.

I opened my mouth to speak, but that was when the first Drainer broke from around the corner of the tunnel.

25-CHAPTER

He stopped so abruptly that the other two following ran into him, one after the other, like some scene from the *Three Stooges*, all three of his black eyes wider than one would have thought possible.

In his grimy hand, he held what looked like a gray balloon filled with water, the kind we used to throw at each other as kids during the hot summer days. But this was no water balloon. I knew, maybe before they even turned the corner, that it was filled with the knock-out gas that would make the unsavory pile of bones a reality.

No one moved for a split second, and then the lead Drainer (sounds like some kind of metal punk band, right?) raised his arm.

"Arzur?" I said.

Have you ever seen something out of the corner of your eye, turned, and saw there was nothing there? That was how quickly Arzur did what he did. I only felt the stir of stale air as he went to work.

The heads of the three Drainers were lying at their feet after bouncing off of the identical gashes on their three-nippled chests before any of them had actually hit the dirt.

He turned back to me, bowed at the waist, smiled, and then raised the balloon, still intact, over his head while it rested in his upper left hand.

"That was not so difficult, Seer. Perhaps we—"

The second balloon was still spinning through the air when I saw it in my mind's eye, followed quickly by a second and then a third.

The source of those deadly mini-bombs quickly invaded my mind.

The image of a dozen or more Drainers huddled around the bend in the trail from where the first three had appeared was as clear as HDTV, yet I couldn't see them, at least in the physical sense.

"Run! Dammit, run!" I said.

There was no hesitation. The three of us, Arzur, Sabrea, and I, were already some thirty feet down the path and then ducked behind the next curve before Molek got the picture and sprinted to catch up.

I thought I had spoken. In reflection, I realized that I hadn't. The Triad link the three of us shared had worked its magic, but Molek hadn't heard my voice inside his head.

Still, he was making up the distance between us as the first gas bomb thumped the hardened path and disintegrated, releasing the poison from within.

"You'd better hurry your ass, Molek. That stuff isn't going to be good for your future," I said, trying to hide my concern.

His strides grew longer, his smile wider, even as the gas rolled in our direction. It was like we were a magnet for that junk.

"I believe my future lasts a while longer, Seer. Let us all move our asses."

Just then, the platoon of Drainers began to spill into the area we'd just left, maybe only thirty feet behind Molek. The first two in that unholy pack dropped to their knees, and the three behind them fitted long arrows into this world's version of bows, which looked as if they were made from bone, and drew them back.

The former Culroid commander was getting closer to us, but not close enough.

"Come on, Molek, these things aren't fooling around," I urged.

"I am coming."

Ten feet more. He needed ten feet more.

Even in this limited light, I could see the three archers pull back the arrows in perfect sync, determined not to let him cross those remaining few yards.

It was the last act the three archers would consider in this life.

The whir of something rushing over my head sealed the deal for them as three of Sabrea's short metal arrows released from her crossbow in rapid succession, burying themselves into the middle eyes of the three would-be killers one by one.

Another volley and accompanying wind scuttled three more of the Drainers. The others fell back around the stone outcrop, screaming and growling in anger and fear. Mostly fear, I felt.

"Nice shooting, for a female. You missed hitting that last one dead center by a fraction, though," I said without looking back at her.

"Ahh. You are a funny man, Gabriel. Even though no male on this planet is better than your hot blue chick, I will work on my accuracy, just for you."

"I'm honored. And you are hot."

"As you should be. And I'm aware of my appearance."

Molek reached us, but the gas was so close behind him that I could smell the outer fringes of that cloud, which had grown considerably larger as a result of the three smaller bursts of gas joining together.

I scratched my head, literally, on how that could happen. Then I understood . . . because I felt them.

This wasn't just any ordinary inert gas, but instead, millions of microorganisms acting as one. Sort of like tiny bees as they swarmed to the hive. But these creatures existed with the sole purpose of getting inside our bodies. That made them parasites by definition. That created fear in me, by definition, because I knew we couldn't outrun them. That was evident by the way the cloud was picking up speed. Molek was no slow runner, and they had gained on him.

Even if we could stay ahead of them, and I knew how fast Arzur and Sabrea could move, and on the surface of this plane, I had been quite fast myself. But eventually they would overtake us, fill our lungs, and then set us up as blood donors of the most generous sort. I didn't see a way out of this one.

Have I mentioned I hate knowing stuff before it happens?

We couldn't give up, nevertheless. Yeah, like this group would ever do that.

"Let's roll," I said.

I took the lead, and we sped away from the organized haze in fine order, knowing that before we reached that ancient wooden door and what lay behind it, we'd be dead. But like I said, we had to try.

The faster we moved through the tunnel, the more alive I became. I was more focused and more of my Triad's lives journeyed into that focus. I felt more of what they had been through and more of what they were capable of doing.

I didn't think I would tire, as long as I was still breathing anyway, of the intimate insight this gift had given me. It was as if the joining was the beginning. It wasn't just the auras or the intent of their hearts, which is incredibly special, but the pure motivations leading their lives.

I think all of us would agree that pure anything, other than evil, is something to behold.

Arzur was a warrior, but longed to be something else, something better, yet he is loyal to his calling. His training. His—

Wait. His training.

We had reached a twenty-five-foot straightaway, and I stopped.

"What are you doing?" asked Arzur, pulling up beside me.

"Yes. That is a fine question, Gabriel," said Sabrea.

"Indeed," said Molek, breathing a little harder than the rest of us.

"Arzur. You once had to hold your breath for ten minutes under water, right?"

"Yes. That is certainly no difficult task for my people. Why do you ask?"

"You had to train for that by taking deep breaths and releasing them, right?"

"I did. I could extinguish a fire from twenty steps away. The counsel said they had not seen breath such as mine in all of their collective years. I received that as a great honor. But what does that have to do with us now?"

The look in his large eyes hastily changed to one of realization.

"You want me to blow the gas back to where it came from? But that will not last long, Seer. I know that much."

"It will if you do it the way I tell you to . . . if I'm right, that is."

"Do tell more," said Sabrea.

"I want you to push the cloud of living creeps into the wall and consequently into the bender worms. Even if those worms don't like the meal, they just might kill them trying something new. Kind of like tasting liver to see if you like it," I said.

"Liver? You eat liver on your plane? And I thought we had barbaric traditions," said Sabrea, scrunching up her beautiful face.

"Hey. You people eat guts from desert snakes."

She raised her head high. "Snake guts are a delicacy. On the other hand, livers remove toxins from the body, and yet you would ingest such an organ?"

She had me there.

Before I could answer, the transparent green fog that had been following us entered the area where we had stopped.

"The left wall is brighter. More worms. Force the fog to the left wall."

Arzur took the position to the right of the path, kneeling his nine-foot body as close to the wall as possible for a better angle.

Sabrea and I joined him. Molek followed a few seconds later.

I found myself taking a larger than life gulp of stale air as the others joined me in that exercise. Yet, none of the rest of us matched the substantial intake of oxygen drawn in by my warrior brother. At one point, I wondered if the vacuum he'd created would suck us into his massive chest. That effort made me try harder, and I raked in another breath, absolutely filling my own lungs.

I had no illusions that I would be able to accomplish what Arzur could, but I *knew* every little bit would help.

"Wait for my signal," I said.

The cloud grew closer. Fifteen feet.

It's lime-green color intensified because the parasites had banded closer together in attack mode.

Ten feet, and the first entrails of the sweet-and-sour scent began to reach my nostrils.

A microsecond later, the living haze was in perfect position, and I released a yell, mostly for Molek's benefit. The others knew exactly what to do and when to do it.

"Now!"

With all of the effort my Triad plus one could conjure, we let 'er loose, as they say.

The timing couldn't have been any more precise. The cloud from hell was mere feet from our collective faces when hurricane Arzur came ashore.

At first, I feared I was mistaken.

Imagine that, Gabe Stark, seer, making a booboo at this critical moment.

After the cloud, in its dense entirety, had ricocheted into the brightest section of the wall, it began to reform, releasing a miniscule buzzing sound I'd not noticed from them beforehand. I think they were pissed at being dust in the wind. (I love that song, by the way.)

The gas returned to its original appearance, more intense in color and purpose than before, if that were possible, and then hesitated as if getting its bent-on-destruction bearings. It came right for us.

Six feet away, the first sounds reminded me of popping corn in the microwave.

The parasite fog stopped in its airborne tracks, the next round of popping more intense and accompanied by tiny green flashes of light reminiscent of the display seen in the old *Star Trek* series from the sixties right after they'd fired up the transporter.

Soon, the whole cloud danced in shimmering micro-explosions so intense that I expected Spock and Kirk to come flying though, Bones complaining and bringing up the rear.

Then, as quickly as it began, it was over.

No buzzing, no motion, no transparent cloud of death or anything similar. It was only us chickens and the bender worms who had just saved our butts.

I love it when a plan comes together.

"It appears that your intuition was of some use this time, Gabriel Stark," said Sabrea, smothering me with a hug that pressed my face into her substantial breasts and laughing like she does.

I'm pretty sure I've mentioned how much I missed Kara. I *really* missed her after that embrace.

"Okay, okay, just let me loose."

"You do not like my attempt at affection and gratitude?"

"Nope. I love it."

"You do not like my, how do you say, melons?"

"I love melons, but those aren't Kara's."

She held me out at arm's length. "She is a lucky female. I pray we live long enough that I might meet her."

I contemplated that situation for a moment. I didn't know how that could happen, at least in the terms of the realms that separated us and the ever-present danger therein. *If* I did get out alive, never mind what would happen once I opened my mouth about any of this to Kara. She'd say something like "bless your heart" and call the on-duty psychiatrist.

"I wish that as well," said Arzur.

"I as much as your Triad," said Molek.

His emotion made me turn my head. He had let his guard down a fraction, and I felt something from him that I'd not detected before, an emotion wholly unexpected.

There was a longing of acceptance, and maybe even love, in that brief glimpse into this human turned Culroid and back to human. And it was for me alone.

Why?

I shook my head. No time to consider all that.

The loud, obtrusive report of wood colliding against wood made that so.

We'd run so far and so fast that we didn't realize how close we were to the very door that had led us to this path.

Whirling toward the sound, I saw we were mere steps from the very first bend we had traveled around when we'd sought refuge and escape.

There was another egregious thump accompanied by a loud, unified squeal of glee by what sounded like hundreds of voices.

Our time had run out. The Master's legion would be through the door any moment now.

26-CHAPTER

"What should we prepare for, Seer?" asked Arzur, drawing his swords.

I was about to answer him when I was interrupted by another loud crack that shook the very ground, yet it seemed farther away than the last one.

I closed my eyes and concentrated on the sound's origin. It didn't take long to decipher where the ruckus was truly coming from and why we were mistaken.

What do you know? We had gotten a sliver of a break, if you think a brief respite from the Master's army a break.

"Seer?' asked Sabrea.

I turned to the three of them.

"The pounding is so loud we thought it was at this door, but it isn't. They are trying to get through the entrance that led us to the chamber of our joining."

"So there is no one outside that door? How can it be? I can hear them. I can even smell the Culroids," said Arzur.

"It's a trick. A deception by the Master, I think."

Molek nodded. "I have seen such trickery before. You are correct, Gabriel."

"But it won't be long before they break through. We need to get back into this chamber and try to get outside," I said.

"The only other exit is the timeworn, unstable stairs that lead upward toward the surface," said Sabrea. "They did not look strong enough to withstand the burden of our weight."

"They will," I said.

"Let us go then," said Arzur.

He took a few strides and pushed on the door. It held fast.

Arzur pushed again, the muscles in his arms turning to something the Hulk would have been proud of, as the door groaned. He backed up, lowered his right shoulder, and began his charge.

The door had no chance. I watched as it exploded into dozens of shards of ancient wood, leaving little left of what had been there for centuries. Arzur tumbled through the new entrance.

He stood there, the grin on his face wide.

"We don't need no stinkin' key," he said, mimicking a strong New York City accent.

I laughed loudly.

"Where did you learn that accent?"

"Oh, from your head, Seer. Even though you still don't fully trust what you are, I do, and at times, I can hear your thoughts speak to me. I know that this strange manner of speech makes you laugh. Does it not?"

"Why do want to make me laugh?"

"I like the sound of it, and I like to feel your mirth as well. I am a warrior first, but my heart is large for other things, as you have seen."

"I have seen that. And thank you. You can practice your Al Pacino voice later, however. We need to get our asses out of here."

Ninety seconds later, we stood at the entrance of the stairwell. I pulled down the two red X signs and gave the steps a look.

They spiraled up some forty feet to what appeared to be another thick, wooden door.

The cracks in the old wooden steps, several of them warped and broken, did little to encourage positive thoughts of scaling them swiftly, if at all. Plus, even if the rest of us could make it up, Arzur couldn't.

There was no way any of these planks would hold his weight. He had tremendous leaping ability, but twenty feet was about his limit.

Another triple curse came out of my mouth.

"You are becoming quite good at that," said Sabrea.

"I've had more practice lately," I answered.

The renewed pounding reflected the attempt of the Master's throng to enter this chamber. It got our attention as it grew closer. Much closer. They had succeeded in getting into the room on the other side of the door that Molek had reinforced with a steel rod.

Their combined purpose was startlingly clear. They meant to tear us apart and pick their teeth with our bones, after cooking us to their desired temperature.

I hadn't contemplated or sensed their cannibalistic tendencies until this moment. That, or denial was still a luxury for me.

Swinging back to the stairwell, I then looked at my companions.

"We need to try this. Now."

"If you say so, Seer," said Sabrea, her eyes boring into mine.

"If the three of us can get to the top, we can figure out how to get Arzur up to open the door and—"

I stopped, realizing how stupid I sounded.

Did I think there was a hidden crane up there? Dumbass.

Arzur's thoughts broke into mine.

"Trust yourself, Gabriel. We all do."

He hadn't referred to me as Gabriel, only Seer, since we'd met. I took this last reference as meaning something more than Triad partners.

We were friends.

That statement is powerful when one dwells on it. Not acquaintances or drinking pals, not teammates even, but friends who understood and loved each other in ways that others simply didn't understand. It was sort of like being married without the sex.

Thank God.

Wisdom is a fickle woman, hiding her face and daring one to find out what she looks like. I think I just met her, however.

For maybe the first time since I'd arrived in this world, I truly understood what Sabrea and Arzur had been trying to say to me about my seeing ability.

None of it was about knowing my people inside and out, or them knowing me. Not about the joining that made that knowledge even clearer. Not about auras or knowing the intent of one's heart.

Even though those things were important, they weren't why we were here or who we were.

Our journey was about the greater good. About doing what it took, giving what we each had, to make things right. About protecting the ideal that Ben had alluded to when he pointed out that it was more important for the masses to grasp the concept of doing right things than the embodiment of such ideals in a single person.

In short, it ain't about me or my tiny world as I understand it. What we do, how we act, should always be about others first. The rest will take care of itself.

I'd been more self-centered than I'd realized. Funny how we think we're really good people, then discover there are a few chinks in that armor of thought. I had more than a few.

That was now over.

The next moment, what we had to do became perfectly clear.

About damn time.

"You have something to say?" asked Sabrea, her face glowing.

I reached up and kissed her on the lips, then watched as she grinned even wider.

"What was that for, Gabriel?"

"It's in case we don't make it, which I see we probably won't. I wanted you to know what it was like to kiss someone who loves you."

"Thank you," she whispered, knowing full well what I meant. "My love is strong for you as well, even though we shan't lie naked."

Motioning for Molek and Arzur to stand next to her, I then stepped away and bowed to them in the way I'd seen Arzur greet Sabrea.

"I'm honored to be in your company," I said. "I would die for you all."

Arzur cleared his throat while Molek wiped at his eyes as we shook hands, all of them.

"Just do not kiss us," said Arzur.

"I won't. You two aren't as pretty."

"I'm grateful that you noticed," said Arzur.

There was another nerve-shattering crash as more of the door was destroyed.

"So do you have a plan?" asked Molek.

"Yep. This is what we are going to do."

I brought my Triad plus one close to me, wrapped my arms around all of them as much as their combined sizes would allow, and let them in on the next step of our journey . . . as their seer saw it.

27-CHAPTER

So here we are. I've caught you up to date, right up to the minute, in fact, as we await the battle of a lifetime. Needless to say, we are great underdogs here.

What we are about to do, or not do, is going to hinge on the next measure of time and my trust in the fate that brought me into Sabrea's plane.

I wasn't lying when I said we didn't have much of that precious commodity, time. None of us, including those on other planes. I suppose that means you as well.

I pray that our decision here will make a difference. If not, we'll know soon enough.

Here goes.

There was no mistaking the fact that there were agents of the Master giving their perverted best to get through the door that led to the joining chamber where we waited. This gate, twelve-feet across by maybe twenty-feet high, was all that separated us from a certain death. I think the oddsmakers would have us going down in under ten minutes.

They would probably be right, but what the hell, I'd never wanted to know the odds anyway.

"Open it."

Molek nodded and then put his hand on the metal rod, preparing to pull it away from the door.

No, we're not crazy. Well, maybe a little, but you know that.

I had explained my plan, fueled by insight, to the others, and it seemed to make sense. Right up until I gave the order to remove the rod.

The sweat oozing from every pore on my body verified my doubt.

My logic had been that we could defend a doorway of this size far better than getting to the surface, if we even got that far, and then giving our enemies the opportunity to attack from the air and surrounding us, overwhelming us by sheer numbers.

We were about to test that theory.

Molek looked back at me as he prepared to pull the rod out of the slot.

"You must stand behind Arzur and Sabrea. I will take the right side as planned, but you cannot move in front of me or the others, Seer. Do not forget what your gift truly is," Molek warned.

"Yeah, yeah. We've been through this. I get it." I glanced at the ornate sword in my hand.

"He is right, Gabriel," said Sabrea. "Molek and I are to be Arzur's wing male and female while he battles the main flow of Culroids. Your plan, remember?"

"I said I get it. Now do it. Our timing here is critical."

That part was true.

Our chance of survival was better at that minute than at any other, and that was only poor at best. I didn't let the others in on that, but I suspected none of them needed me to figure that out. And, as a side note, if any of my companions thought that I was going to stay out of the fray, they were nuts. They probably knew that too.

Sabrea gave me a side glance accompanied by a magnificent wink. I had to smile despite our situation.

The metal rod then hit the dirt floor, and Molek jumped to his right. I stepped back behind Arzur, who stood ready with a marvelous sword in each of his upper hands.

Nothing happened.

The door remained closed, and the activity on the other side had suddenly stopped in almost perfect sync to Molek's pulling the rod.

I felt no vibes, no aura, only the sense of ultimate evil. I honed in on why the Culroids weren't attacking.

Shit. Immediately I knew the Master was blocking me, almost completely.

That fact explained a couple of things regarding why I couldn't read everything all of the time. Even so, I felt my ability growing. The Master wouldn't be able to keep things from me forever.

I concentrated harder. Each second that passed was allowing more of the Master's horde to gain access to the outer chamber. But I needed to know why they weren't attacking.

I searched with all of my being, but I couldn't even tell what time of day it was outside.

Then it hit me.

Molek.

He'd been cleansed of the Master's control, but he was still linked to her, even though I'd believed he wasn't. Damn it.

But the solution came quickly.

"Molek. Clear your thoughts and think only of home or dogs or old girlfriends or whatever. Anything other than this battle."

"I do not understand."

"Let me make this brief. The Master still has a link with you, no matter what we believe. I think that's why they are not attacking. She may sense what you are up to, at least on some level. Got it?"

"I get it."

He closed his eyes and did his best to think about other things. I hoped whatever link he still had would break and show that we were no longer in this room, forcing their hand. The Master simply couldn't afford for us to get away again.

Molek wasn't completely successful, but close enough.

Almost immediately the doors slammed open, and the party began in earnest.

I took a step back, even though I knew what to expect.

The odor was horrific, and the sound of war screams deafening. And talk about ugly.

None of that fazed Arzur, and he held no compunction to hesitate.

I took another step back as the blood had already begun to flow, covering the wall, the ground, and us. Green blood at that.

Arzur was like a machine as he waded into the Culroids. I barely saw the swords as they churned death and destruction.

The leaders of the charge tried to crowd through the door, but not more than eight or ten could enter at one time. Those odds were awful— for the Culroids.

I suspect Arzur could have done what he was doing while reading a book with one hand and sipping tea with one of the others. It was simply no contest.

The bodies were piling up so quickly that Arzur had begun to kick them from the doorway back into the outer chamber—in between slicing sessions. I watched some of those bodies fly twenty feet into the air and land against the far wall.

Molek and Sabrea stood at the ready, but neither needed to use their swords. At one point, Sabrea sheaved hers and pulled out her bow. Good move.

We'd talked about the flying monsters, the Argats, making an entrance at some point and even though Arzur could reach them, there was a better chance of one of them getting through in the air than on the ground. And she needed to be on the ready in the event that a burst saber or two showed up.

Molek had told us this army didn't have many of the burst sabers; there simply were not many in existence, and it wouldn't be advantageous to them if one were to fall into our hands. I found myself wishing we'd kept the one that Molek had wanted to fry me with.

Five minutes in and, by my estimate, over a two-hundred dead Culroids later, the flow begun to subside as our logic began to show itself as real. The would-be harvesters of our lives simply could not get into the room quickly enough to complete their mission.

They hadn't even forced Arzur to breathe hard or any of the rest of us to lift a hand, for that matter.

That suddenly changed.

I sensed the explosion from behind me just before it rattled the room and more. My teeth felt as if they would vibrate right out of my mouth.

I hoped not. I hate dentists.

Turning toward the sound, I did so in time to see a flow of light from the top of the stairs where the old door had once resided. The opening then darkened into strange, fluttery patterns, and the room began to fill with Argats.

I thought the Culroids were dangerous.

I made a quick decision, not totally unexpecting this maneuver.

It is what I would have done.

"Arzur. You need to keep doing what you're doing. The rest of us will handle this."

"As you wish," he said, not turning his head while taking out another half dozen Culroids who had picked up the pace of the attack again.

Molek and Sabrea were by my side instantly, and I heard that familiar sound of short arrows burrowing through the air.

I watched as two of the flying demons with the pleasant faces bit the dust, thanks to Sabrea's crossbow.

She lit up three more, and then we charged the area.

Even though Molek and Sabrea moved to my flanks, they left room for me to come up the middle. I felt like Barry Sanders doing one of those fantastic runs to the end zone.

We reached the bottom of the rickety steps as several more Argats entered the chamber.

Three more fell to the earth with steel arrows lodged deep into their throats.

Only about a hundred and a quarter to go.

"How many arrows left?" I asked, both hands on my sword, looking upward.

"Several, but surely not enough," answered Sabrea.

"What do we do?" asked Molek.

"We wait. They'll come to us," I said.

We didn't have to wait long.

In perfect sync, three of them joined together to form a small flying wall, pointed tales curled beneath their scaly bodies, diving in our direction.

"Down," I yelled.

We did just that, lowering our backs only inches from each other.

The three tails swept toward us. I felt like a row of corn about to be cultivated. I now had more compassion for weeds.

Just as the tails, hanging a few feet below the owners' bodies, reached us, three swords rose together.

A harmony of screams followed as the tails were disarticulated from their hostesses, sending all three crashing into the side wall, losing the precious balance that the tails provided them in flight.

"I've got this," I said.

I felt Sabrea's hand fall from my back as I beat the other two to my feet and raced to the wall.

"Wait," pleaded Molek.

Hell no. I was tired of waiting.

I reached the wall and promptly drove my sword into the chest of the first Argat. I drew Goldie (my clever new name for my sword) out of the first demon and repeated my actions a second time.

I rushed to the third one eagerly, ready to earn the trifecta, when I heard the crash of body on dirt from behind.

Sabrea had nailed another of the flying wenches. That was good. But by doing so, the body got me from behind.

That was bad.

In a blink, I was hit in the back of my legs and flew forward directly into the not so sexy lap of the third Argat, my sword loosened from my hands, tumbling to the ground.

You know that song that says something about not being able to please everyone? Well, she wasn't happy to see me or maybe she didn't like my butt on her scaly chest.

Go figure.

While she and her dead comrades had lost substantial strength and life force, they were still a force to be reckoned with.

The Argat's version of hands swiftly closed around my head as she forced me toward those sharp teeth designed for tearing flesh.

Her breath was as sickening as you might imagine. I guess that has to do with the rotted meat draped over a few of her pearly not-so-whites.

Did anyone in this place brush their damned teeth?

I strained against her with all of my strength, but I was losing the battle.

Millimeter by millimeter, I was getting closer to having my face redesigned. I guess the good thing was that no matter what happened here, I'd still look better than Mickey Rourke.

I was only an inch away and I saw her smile. I renewed my effort and gained some ground, but I knew it was almost over. If the bite didn't kill me, the poison she would inject into my system surely would.

She pulled with a replenished effort, and I was suddenly so close to her that I could have licked her lips.

I closed my eyes.

I thought I'd get back to Kara at some point, but I always knew death was a possibility, didn't I?

I found myself begging for just one more kiss, one more night alone with her. But it seemed as if destiny and this bitch had different plans.

There was a hissing sound as I was abruptly sent backward by the force of my pulling effort, rocking against the creature I was sitting on as I did.

Molek lifted me from her body, blood dripping from his sword, and handed me my Goldie.

"Your fate is not determined by these creatures," he said.

That was good to hear.

"Thank you, my friend."

"We are more than friends, Gabriel. Surely you have seen that."

I frowned.

I had no idea what he was talking about. Or did I?

I had no more time to think about his words as another wave of Argats zeroed in on the two of us.

Sabrea, in all of her glory, didn't allow them to get close, and into the dirt they fell, bleeding, impaled, unmoving. That's a great combo for the good guys.

"Come this way. We will fight from this corner. I have but six arrows left, and there are far more of these flying heifers than six to deal with."

"Heifers?" I asked.

"Yes. I like that word, Gabriel."

She didn't have to tell me twice.

We ran to her side with every intention of backing up to the corner to the left of the hole the throng of the Master had blown into the door. That would protect our backs, at least.

I didn't make it.

My foot caught on something, and I went down in a heap, the sound of metal on metal ringing in my ears as my left leg banged into something.

I rolled over and came face to face with manna from heaven.

Old Gabe had tripped over a burst saber.

I hadn't noticed if one of the Argats was carrying it or not when Sabrea dropped them from the air, but frankly, Scarlett . . .

Maybe Ben or Samuel were watching over us after all.

I grabbed the saber, which was lighter than I thought it would be, and raised it high in both hands, felt for the trigger that I'd seen Molek reach for when he was ready to turn me golden brown, and promptly fired it at one of the flying scags.

The explosion was gratifying, her scream orgasmic. Well, you get the picture.

"Seer. Give that to me. I can—"

"No way," I said, cutting off Molek in midsentence. "I've got this. You two are better in hand-to-hand. You swing the swords, and I'll blow the junk from their trunks."

He laughed out loud.

"Your logic is sound, Gabriel."

I took two more flying hussies out before chancing a look toward Arzur and the door.

The pile of Culroids was incredibly high as a result of his handiwork. Their bloodied bodies looking like a glimmering field of green were now blocking the entrance to this chamber almost completely.

His workload was quickly diminishing because they couldn't get to him. He must have killed five or six hundred of them, at least.

Samson had nothing on my warrior companion.

I turned back to our fight, fully confident that Arzur would be joining us soon and not just because he had no one else to slay. I had an unexpected pang of knowledge that the battle had not gone the horde's way, and they were concerned about actually losing the battle, which would greatly affect their domination plans.

Hey, you know what? They *were* getting their collective asses kicked.

They were the grass, and we were the lawnmowers.

I felt a sudden burst of pride and confidence. Our plan was working, we'd gotten a couple of breaks, and the Master was having doubts. The only thing that could make this better was a fat hamburger and a beer.

The flow of Argats continued, but their aggressiveness dwindled with each new death, breaking a very basic rule of battle. In short, they were losing heart. And we were gaining it.

We fought on with determined purpose.

At one point, I gave Molek the saber, and I stood back to back . . . well, back to butt with

Sabrea, and flashed my sword with ever-increasing proficiency.

No, I'm not a warrior in the vein that Arzur is, or even Sabrea or Molek. But the knowledge they had shared verbally and mind to mind had a profound effect on my physical prowess. Throw in a metal leg that would make Steve Austin green with envy, and I wasn't half bad at defending myself and Sabrea's shapely backside.

One more slash-and-re-slash party, hosted by yours truly, had left two more Argats on the floor of the chamber. The flying vermin were now gone, out-of-the-blue gone.

They had hightailed out of this death trap, those that were left. The sound of flapping wings and blood-curdling screams was abruptly absent.

I twisted toward the doors and watched as Arzur closed them, replaced the rod, and then jogged our way.

He was covered in tangled guts and green blood, his swords reflecting the same. Those attributes were in stark contrast to his bright teeth as they shined in a smile he wore from ear to ear.

I could hardly believe it.

We had done it. The four of us, just four, had driven back a host of forty-eight hundred beings led by a leader who stood for everything we did not.

It then occurred to me that it hadn't been simply the four of us. The hand of those opposed to evil had been a part of our victory in ways I didn't quite understand, but I was getting closer. Collective faith and righteousness. Is there such a state?

The four of us converged, Arzur dropping to his knees so we could reach him, arms around shoulders, laughing and talking all at once.

"Your plan was brilliant, Seer," said Arzur. "I hardly worked up an appetite."

"Oh shucks, it weren't nothing."

"It was something, Gabriel. Very much something. Are you positive you don't want to lay with me? I will explain it to your wife, if you desire."

"Okay. I'll do it."

Her jaw dropped. Then she caught on, smiling sheepishly.

"You got me, Seer. Yes, you did."

"Paybacks," I said.

"Yes, but remember what I said about never lying."

"I do remember."

"Know this. You will see me naked, Gabriel."

We stared at each other, than she threw back her head, laughing. "I can play that game, Seer."

I sighed with relief, almost.

"Yeah, you can. But let's play it later. I love how winning feels."

"It feels outstanding, but joking aside, she is right. We executed the plan, but your logic, and your warrior portion was magnificent," said Molek.

I tilted my head and looked at him. His tone was more than complimentary. It was as if he was, I don't know, proud of me.

"Thank you, all of you, but we did this together. This Triad plus one did what the Master was afraid we would do. We turned them back and are still alive, much to her chagrin. It doesn't get any better—"

A moment later, I was on my knees, the screaming pain inside my head forcing my eyes into a black void. Then as quickly as it had come, the pain left. The black void did not.

That's where she stood, directly in the middle of that thick darkness. I wasn't in the chamber with my comrades any longer because it had been swallowed up by her essence.

By her, I mean there was no mistaking the red cloak and the feminine shape beneath that cloak.

The Master had come a'calling and without an invitation.

She stepped purposefully to me, bent down and lifted my chin with long fingers supporting two-inch nails.

"You believe you have won, Seer? You think that you have defeated me by killing a thousand of my warriors?"

I couldn't see her face, but that voice was unmistakable.

I'm sure my eyes widened. At least I kept my mouth closed.

Dr. Nadia Thomas addressed me without the Caribbean accent.

My mind ran back to the first time I'd met her, realizing that she had been a wolf in sheep's clothing. She'd never had an aura really, only that area of darkness that held the shape of an aura.

Oh, if I'd known then what I know now.

I gathered my composure and did what I do, that or faint.

"Hey, Doc, and yes, I do think we've won this one. We kicked your evil ass here."

With her other hand, she pulled the hood from her face and head, revealing that same shit-eating grin I'd seen when she came into my hospital room for the first time.

"I see that you still need to put on, like, thirty pounds."

That smile grew even wider revealing two rows of sharp, white teeth.

"And how should I do that? Should I eat my fill?"

I went cold inside, her meaning perfectly clear. I didn't answer her.

"Oh, no smartass remark to that one?"

I still held my tongue, not totally sure why, just knowing it was the right thing to do.

Silence was golden in this instance. It was better for my health and that of my Triad.

Her eyes searched my face, her head tilting to one side and then another.

"You do well to listen to your gift and to keep silent. But I still require a true answer. Do you think you've defeated me?"

Under the circumstances, I should have answered her again. I should have rubbed it in that I believed we had. Yet, the old adage of never asking a question that you didn't know the answer to flashed into my thoughts. She knew something I didn't. I got that much.

I didn't speak.

She stood upright, waved her hand, and I was up and off my feet, literally.

"I do not have patience. I will give you one more chance to answer me."

I looked at my boots, still covered with Argat blood. What we had done was real. The blood was proof. She had somehow managed to bring me to her dimension and out of my reality, but I didn't have to stay. I knew that much.

I closed my mind to her influence and drew upon the strength of my Triad. And in case you haven't noticed, there was some mojo there.

It was enough.

Slowly, I settled to the floor of wherever we were, my eyes not leaving her face.

She blinked and stepped back, cursing me in a language I didn't understand.

She snarled as her eyes began to protrude. Her jaw followed suit as her snout became far more that of a wolf than a human. She grew taller, larger, stronger, and more unpleasant to look at as her skin turned into a scaly black, those protruding eyes evolving into red coals of hate and pure—and I mean pure—malevolence.

Strangely, I wasn't frightened of her appearance. Her intent, well, that was something of a different world, but I had an anchor on which to hold.

She knew that, and for the second time since I'd met this entity, I sensed a sort of fear from her. That fact made me a shade cocky.

"I'll say it again. You lost this one, Doc. I know you never wanted me to meet my comrades and certainly not to join. But we did, and we won the first battle. I know that scares you down to your black heart."

I stepped forward. "Doesn't it?"

Her unexpected laugh shook me to the core. I hate that.

"You do not understand, even now, do you? Fear? Perhaps you should refine your abilities before you say such things."

"Maybe, but you can't bluff your way out of what I see in you. Perhaps you should get a grip on that, wench."

"You see nothing that I didn't allow."

"Yeah, that's what they all say."

"I am not all."

With a sudden jerk of her head to the side, she raised her ear as if listening to something that I couldn't hear.

This time, there was no mistaking her angst. Something or someone had gotten her undivided attention.

She turned back to me.

"I must go. I have other concerns in other locations. But before I go, I will give you one last message as proof to the folly of your unfruitful 'win' as you call it. We will meet again."

The flick of her fingers was all I saw, and I was instantly back in the midst of my people. I breathed a sigh of relief.

"You left us again, Gabriel," said Sabrea. "It is getting old."

"Sorry. I didn't choose that vacation site."

"Was it the Master? Was it she who beckoned you?" asked Molek anxiously.

"Yeah, it was. So did I actually leave here?"

"Yes, this time you were gone. In the cavern, you slept as you visited the realm of the Drainers," said Sabrea.

I frowned at that. I just assumed that I was seeing things in my mind and was in some sort of trance-like state. So did that mean—?

The bloodcurdling scream interrupted my thoughts.

I turned my eyes upward and saw the Argat, bigger than the rest we had killed, bearing down on me, her tail slung low in attack mode.

In an instance, I knew I had no time to dodge her. She was coming too fast, and Arzur and Sabrea would not be able to help, in spite of their athletic prowess. It was as if we'd all been put under a slow-motion spell. The Master's work, no doubt.

Quick deductions were my forte. I hated this one.

The Master was right. I hadn't won shit. In the end, I was only going to be another dead seer.

I really wanted to grow old.

Only a few feet away from me, I saw something flash in front of the Argat.

Molek.

He hit her with a tackle that would have made Dick Butkus proud, sending them both yards away from me. But a second later, he paid the price for his heroism as her rigid tail drove into his stomach and exited through his back at the precise moment they hit the dirt.

"No!" I yelled, recovering enough to scramble to my feet.

I ran to where the two of them thrashed on the ground, getting to them at the same time as Arzur and Sabrea, pulling my sword as I ran.

Molek saw me, flipped the winged beast on her side, and I cleaned her head from her shoulders, spattering myself with blood in the process. I watched as Arzur severed her body from her tail and then kicked her to the other side of the room.

I fell at Molek's side, dropping Goldie and then pulled the tail from my impaled friend.

I put both hands over the gushing flow of blood, trying to prevent the unpreventable.

"You dumbass. Why did you do that?" I asked, tears already running over my cheeks.

I didn't care about my tears.

He focused on my face, his eyes now a blue that matched my own.

"You ask such a question?" he said softly.

"Yes. I was ready to die for this cause. I knew the risks."

He coughed, blood spraying from his mouth.

"You were, and that is noble, but your destiny is far more complicated and necessary, Gabriel."

I felt Sabrea and Arzur's hands on my shoulders as I released more tears while this brave man's life force ebbed.

"I'm not more important than you," I argued.

"Ahh, but you are. Your work has only begun. Besides, what father wouldn't die for his son?"

"What?" said Sabrea.

Arzur said nothing.

Molek's words should have stunned me, but they didn't. He'd done his best to hold that back from me until now, but I already knew it. I knew it.

He was the tall, good-looking man who had met Mother Mary in that bar those years ago. He had intentions of seeing her again, but the very next day, had been drawn into this war and taken against his will from our world into this one. Captured, tortured, and forced to serve a realm he didn't want to serve. That spark of defiance and determination had been what had, in the end, saved him and brought him to me.

He coughed again, and I released my hands from his belly.

We looked into each other's eyes and souls, finding some peace in that.

I had so many emotions running through my thoughts, but realized I'd have to sort them later. I had no choice.

Leaning to him, I kissed him on the forehead.

"Thank you, Father."

He reached up with a weak hand, caressed my cheek, smiled, and then Molek my father, this man returned from the world of the Culroids and my would-be killer, died.

28-CHAPTER

Arzur handed Molek's sword to me, and I drove it into the ground at the head of his grave located beneath the band of three trees situated on the south side of the small oasis near where we'd exited the pit of death.

Funny how that chamber had run the full gauntlet of good, evil, victory, defeat . . . all in the span of a few hours. It reflected life, and my time with Molek, in a very real way.

I had no true feelings for him as a father, not really. Probably less than for Mother Mary as my biological mother, even though I knew both situations were true. But as a friend, a comrade, I'd learned to love him in just a matter of hours. His sacrifice justified that love, a million times over. His grasp of the big picture had been better than mine.

He knew that our Triad had to stay together for the greater good. Deep down, I suppose I knew that was true, but knowing such things and then watching another practice that unselfishness was another matter entirely. He had given up everything, and I was grateful. He'd even helped me accept my gift more readily by expressing his trust.

What else can I say about a man who died so that I could live?

I glanced up at the sun hanging low in the sky, feeling its perfect warmth, the beginning images of two moons low on the horizon beyond it.

Soon it would shine on Molek's grave. I thought that appropriate. He was no longer a creature of the dark.

"Are you well, Seer?" asked Arzur.

"Yeah, I'm okay. Molek is at rest, and there is a great peace regarding that."

"If any one deserved such peace, it is he," said Sabrea.

"I agree," I whispered.

With that, she bowed in the grave's direction. Arzur followed, then I.

"Rest well, comrade. May the light keep you until we meet again," said Sabrea.

"May it be true," said Arzur.

"Here, here," I said.

My two friends rose and moved to my side.

"She, the Master, shall pay for this," said Arzur.

"She will. Count on it. She said we'd meet again, and you can bank on that. We whooped her ass, and she didn't like it. She is worried about us. She wanted to send one last message by destroying the Triad. She hadn't counted on Molek . . . and his sacrifice," I said softly.

"She did not. Nor did she suspect that this world would oppose her as we have. She has lost the battle here, at least for the moment," said Sabrea.

"There's that," I said.

"Even though none joined us in this battle, my mind knows that we fought in different places and in different ways. My plane is safe for now."

She was right on all accounts. Ben had been right. Collective good had won this one.

But had we truly saved this version of Earth, or merely delayed the inevitable?

I think the truth is somewhere between "saved" and "could still be in deep doo-doo," but right now, the good guys were on top. That meant something.

Sabrea and Arzur stood next to me as we took one more long, drawn-out look at the sun.

I know we had only been underground for a few hours, but that darkness had threatened to replace the light inside each of us. Not all darkness is exposed by the light. Some stays deep inside, if you allow it.

We hadn't.

"We have been through much already, Seer, and you have grown in your acceptance and trust in your gift, have you not?" asked Sabrea.

"I have. I at least know why it doesn't work all of the time, I suppose. It's up to me to believe and channel what it can do. I can control seeing auras and understand what others are intending. I can see the future at times, and I know you two better than myself, but I've also learned that this gift is a gentleman, in that it will respect privacy. I also know it can protect us."

"This is all true, but we need for it to do something else. For *you* to do something else," said Sabrea.

I didn't answer; I didn't want to just yet. Instead, I went to Molek's grave and saluted.

After touching his sword a final time, we climbed up the grassy hill of the oasis and stood on the tallest dune, touching each other arm to arm . . . well, only one of Arzur's.

"You both are wondering what's next, right?" I asked.

"Yes," said Arzur.

Good question.

I wondered what Kara was thinking right now. Did I want to know?

I questioned if I'd see her or the farm or Apollo again. My heart ached at the prospect of never doing any of those things again, but not touching my wife in every way topped the list of hellish endurance.

I could will myself back to her and that bed. I know it. But that wasn't in the cards right now, and we must all play the hand we're dealt. Ask Kenny Rogers.

With swift recollection, the words that Nurse Peggy said I'd been reciting came back to me.

Your choice will impact everything, but either way, I love you.

Kara. Those words were Kara's.

She must have known about what was coming. Dreams? A soul link between the two of us? A *Jeopardy* question? I don't know, but I was right.

The urge to leave this plane without even answering Sabrea grew eminently stronger because the vision of Kara grew eminently stronger.

I could go. I wanted to go. I even knew how to go. But then the red-cloaked hussy wins. That wasn't going to happen, no matter my personal cost, not if I could help it. I don't know if that was noble or not, I just knew it was true. We weren't going down without a fight.

Good God, life in any dimension can be hard. I vacillated back and forth, then put Kara, my other life, and even Apollo on the back burners. I reached for my blue Amazon's hand.

"I don't know. I just know this isn't over."

"Are you sure?" asked Sabrea.

"Yeah, I'm sure."

"Why?" asked Arzur.

"Because we and the Master are still alive. She can't handle that."

"Fair enough," said Arzur.

"Enough of this talk. I am hungry and desire drink. Let us go to the next town and feed the beast, as you say," said Sabrea, grinning. "And if I partake of enough liquid pleasure, I will show you my tattoos."

"I would like to see them," said Arzur.

I laughed and stood.

"Me too."

Sabrea led the way down the dune as we pondered what was next.

Whatever it was, we wouldn't be completely safe, but as long as I was with these two, I'd be fine.

I knew that was right.

Even a new seer could see that much.

Thank you for reading the first installment of Seer! The Triad had quite a first adventure.

As I mentioned before, this is the first of three installments. Please let me know what you think of Gabe and his gang.

This was an entirely new adventure for me, and I loved changing gears to this type of story, this genre. I hope you feel the same.

I'll be back to Manny and his crew shortly, their story is far from over, and another installment of Ellen Harper's world, plus a brand-new series that I'm truly excited about.

Yours,

Rick Murcer

rickmurcer@gmail.com
www.rickmurcer.com